GIFTED

THE DARK FORGOTTEN

SHARON ASHWOOD

Cover art by The Illustrated Author.

Edited by Cynthia Shepp.

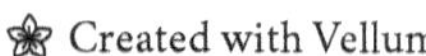 Created with Vellum

PRAISE FOR SHARON ASHWOOD

Sharon Ashwood is all that is good and right in the paranormal romance genre.

— BITTEN BY BOOKS

Fast paced and captivating… chemistry is immediate and undeniable, and the love scenes are scorching hot.

— PUBLISHERS WEEKLY

Multiply the Wow Factor, the Dark Forgotten saga must continue!

— SINGLE TITLES

This is a splendid way to spend your precious leisure time!

— ROMANTIC TIMES BOOK REVIEWS TOP PICK!

DEAR READER

Dear Reader,

What do vampires, werewolves, and witches do for the holidays?

It's a good question, and I found myself answering it more than once. This novella started out as a short story, then became a series of four short stories, which then wove themselves into a connected tale. Think of this as a gossipy ramble through the neighborhood, with added supernatural features. And a festive demon. And Frederick the Unicorn.

To find out specific supernatural holiday plans, you'll need to read on. However—as is the case with us humans—the truth is as varied as the people involved. Family, gifts, desires, and regrets are never simple, and they can often lead us to unexpected places. It doesn't matter if you're a part-time wolf or hundreds of years old. The season can be both a challenge and a glorious joy.

Most of the characters in this holiday story appear in the Dark Forgotten series, so past readers will recognize old friends. If you're new to this world, welcome. This is a great introduction because you don't need to have read any of the other books.

ood evening, listeners, this is your night hostess and favorite pussycat, Errata Jones, coming to you from CSUP, the radio station that puts the super in supernatural. It's frosty tonight on the glorious University of Fairview campus with only four more shopping days until Santa Claws stuffs your stockings.

Four days and four nights until the moment of truth? That hardly seems enough time to wallow in all the gift-giving, party-going, eggnog-drinking mayhem, much less to watch all those sentimental holiday specials. But don't fret, my pets, the Yuletide season is an endurance event, not a sprint. Pace yourselves. There's still New Year's Eve to get through.

ALESSANDRO CARAVELLI, vampire, closed the door before the damp December wind chilled him straight through to his bones. There were things he liked about winter—more darkness, less suntan envy—but none of his kind appreciated the cold.

As sheriff of Fairview, he'd been out keeping order among the town's supernatural citizens. He'd taken the early shift, leaving a contingent of hellhounds to finish out the night. It was almost midnight now, still early enough to enjoy some family time in his largely nocturnal household. Hanging his sword on a hook by the door—it was old school but still the most efficient weapon against things that went bump in the night—he dropped his car keys in the tray on the hall table. A stack of mail waited there—junk, bills, a few seasonal cards. Nobody sent actual letters anymore unless they were—like him—from a time that thought the printing press would never catch on.

Instinctively, he drifted toward the warm, sweetly scented kitchen, mail in hand. There, his partner stood icing festive fangs on a tiny gingerbread bat.

"Hello, sweetheart." He kissed her, tasting sugar and spice on her lips.

"Hi," she said, leaning against him. For a moment, they simply drank each other in.

Holly Carver was a witch, part-time student, professional ghost buster, and the center of Alessandro's universe. She was also, via an exceptional bit of magic he barely understood, the mother of their daughter. Currently, little Robin—wearing flannel pajamas covered with tiny pink werewolves—was wrapped around Holly's knee like a squid. She was just over a year old and toddling, if lurching from one handhold to another qualified as such. Alessandro dropped the mail on the wooden table in the corner and picked up his child, tucking her into the crook of his arm. Squeaking in delight, Robin grabbed a handful of his hair and gave it a sharp tug.

He sat, shifting to balance Robin on his knee. She had her mother's green eyes and dimpled smile, not to mention her formidable will. Pulling his daughter close, he rested his chin on top of her soft hair and watched Holly baking. Her dark hair was pulled back in a ponytail, her elfin features flushed from the heat of the oven behind her. There was a smear of icing on her cheekbone.

It was the perfect domestic scene, despite the strangeness of it

—a vampire and a witch playing house in a neighborhood largely populated by supernatural beings. The university town of Fairview had seen more strange things than even conspiracy theorists could dream up.

"How was your evening?" Holly asked, icing the last of the gingerbread bats.

Alessandro made a noncommittal noise. Having remained still for exactly two seconds, Robin was squirming again. He tried to straighten the bow in her wispy blond hair, which seemed to delight her. No sooner had he tied the ribbon than she pulled it free again. It was becoming a fabulous game—at least to her—and he was reconsidering the ethics of hypnotizing his own child into a submissive trance.

"I ran into Ashe today," Holly said, picking up the conversational burden. "She was asking whether we'd heard from Darak or his friends."

"Should I be nervous when your vampire-slaying sister asks after a pack of rogue vampires?" he asked dryly.

"I don't know. I think they had a few things in common." She shuffled the cookie trays, turning her attention to the next decorating job. There were freshly baked ghosts and broomsticks and little werewolves in mid-howl. She began putting tiny silver balls at the tip of each of the wolves' Santa hats.

"They are both members of Homicidal Mercenaries Anonymous?"

Holly gave him a withering look. "Ashe is retired."

"And I'm a vegetarian."

Alessandro gave up on tidying his child and retrieved the stack of mail. He shuffled through it, pausing when he got to a large red envelope labeled in an elegant script. When he tore it open, he expected a fancy Christmas card. Instead, he found a formal invitation edged in gold and green. "Joe's throwing a Christmas Eve party at his hotel and we're on the guest list."

He held up the invitation to show Holly, just out of reach of Robin's grasping hands.

Holly pushed a lock of hair out of her eyes. "I knew he was up to something."

Before he could ask how she knew, his phone buzzed, making Robin giggle. He pulled the device from his pocket and accepted the call without pausing to see who it was.

"Caravelli," he said in his stern sheriff voice.

"It's Perry," said the caller.

Perry Baker was the son of the local Alpha werewolf. Pack Silvertail was filled with strong males, but Perry was the smart one. He taught computer science and knew his way around most spell books, which amounted to more or less the same thing in Alessandro's mind. "What's up?" he asked.

"You know how I volunteer to drive the bus for Aunt Margaret's seniors' home?" It was a casual question, but there was strain in the young werewolf's voice.

In the background, Alessandro could hear a crash, shouts, and someone swearing. Over it all, Christmas carols warbled from a sound system. "Where are you? It sounds like a bikers' holiday party."

"I'm at the community center. I drove the Silvertail seniors out here for bingo night and some eggnog," Perry said. "Unfortunately, things went sideways. I think we have *your* kind of problem."

Which meant supernatural trouble. Alessandro rose from his chair, setting Robin down once more. Holly shot him a questioning glance, so he put the phone on speaker. "Go on."

"I'm not sure, but I think it might be a minor demon. Or a possessed cartoon unicorn. One that really hates Christmas."

"Say that again?"

"Don't ask. Just come."

By now, Alessandro was in the front hall. He put on his coat and retrieved his sword from the wall. Holly had followed, scooping Robin up on the way and setting the toddler on her hip.

"Do you need my help, too?" Holly asked the werewolf on the phone.

"I think I can take care of this one," Perry said. "Besides, I know babysitters are hard to find at this hour. I just need someone to get these people out of here, so I can banish this thing."

"Do you need supplies?" Holly asked. Worry flooded her expression.

"The center has an emergency kit with some basics, but I could use henbane and St. John's wort. I've been consulting with Grandma Carver."

A picture of Holly's grandmother, feisty but frail enough to need two canes, made Alessandro grip the phone hard enough the plastic creaked. "She's there?" he asked.

"Yup."

Holly stifled a groan, meeting his eyes. Of course the old witch—the term meant literally—would be at bingo night. The community center was only a block over from her apartment building, and Grandma liked to gamble.

"I'll be right there." Alessandro ended the call.

Holly went in search of the herbs Perry needed, working one-handed because Robin fussed every time her mom tried to set her down. "I should be there," Holly said with a frown. "Perry's good at what he does, but I have the most experience with demons."

"Let me check out the situation," Alessandro said. "Once the site is clear of civilians, you and I can always trade places if Perry can't handle it."

Holly nodded. She cuddled Robin, whose heavy eyelids were drooping. "Call me as soon as you can. I need to know you're okay. Grandma, too."

He smiled then, amused and still amazed that someone cared if he came home. He was the luckiest vampire on the planet, and he never took that for granted. He kissed Holly hard, his daughter gently, and left the house at a run.

His Thunderbird sat at the curb, a 1960s red two-door with custom chrome and smoked windows. It got him to the center in ten minutes. Alessandro parked behind a converted school bus with the logo of Pack Silvertail's retirement home stenciled on the side. He got out of the car, retrieved his sword from the trunk, and paused to take stock of the scene before he ventured inside.

The community center was a single-story building made from sand-colored brick that looked gray in the dark. It housed a gymnasium, several recreation rooms, a small theater, and a cafeteria that faced the busy street. Both humans and non-humans used the facility, but only the nocturnal clients would be out this late. Christmas lights glowed along the roofline, reflecting in the puddles of rainwater on the street.

Although the cafeteria was dark, the lights were on in the activity room to the right of the front door, turning the foil banner across the window that said "Happy Holidays" into a wavering silhouette. His vampire hearing caught the carols piping through the building's PA system. "O Come, O Come, Emmanuel" floated in an otherwise-silent night. For an instant, he wondered if the crisis had resolved.

Then a metal chair flew through the window, spilling glass, light, and screams into the street. The chair bounced, soaring several yards into the air before crashing to the ground and skidding across the road. Bolting toward the center, he sprang up the steps and yanked open the door—only to recoil. The stink of a moldering grave rolled over him, mixed with the cloying sweetness of cakes and candy. He bared his teeth and slid inside, his footfalls silent.

The double doors to the activity room stood open to his right. Alessandro stopped to one side of the entrance, pressed close to the wall, and then peered inside. He'd learned long ago not to leap into a danger zone without looking first, even though he itched to barge in, sword flashing.

His first glimpse was of rows of folding tables with stacking chairs lined up behind them. A few of the tables had toppled over. Bingo cards and daubers littered the floor. At the front of the room, a machine tumbled balls inside a glass globe, but the caller was cowering on the floor, arms folded over his balding head. Alessandro recognized him as an employee of the center, but couldn't remember his name. No one was speaking—the babble he'd heard over the phone was gone. Even the screams audible from the street had fallen silent.

The Silvertail seniors huddled at the far end next to an artificial tree, Perry's aunt Margaret guarding them like the Alpha she'd once been. Most were the wolves who had come on the bus —easy to spot since a few were furrier than normal, no doubt due to stress. There were also a handful of hellhounds, a scowling demi-fae, and a few elderly witches. He searched until he found Holly's grandmother. He'd known Hazel Carver since she'd been Holly's age, and needed her to be safe. He finally found her at the edge of the group, and she seemed unhurt. A knot inside him released.

But where was the enemy? An eerie stillness froze the scene like the tableau inside a snow globe, silent except for the bland music. He scanned again, this time noticing a table with coffee and cookies along the far wall, the treats as yet untouched. And then the metal coffee urn began to shudder and float upward, the cord straining a moment before it pulled free of the wall plug. A spatter of coffee slopped onto the floor as it rose. Alessandro slipped inside the doorway to watch as it drifted to the ceiling like an iron filing to a magnet.

And there, circling around the overhead light fixture, was a cloud of rainbow mist. It swirled like a miniature cyclone, swatches of pink, blue, and mauve sparkling like a toy from Robin's closet. Around the edges of the cloud, slime trickled down the walls, leaving streaks of glitter on the worn industrial paint. He suddenly understood Perry's reference to unicorns, but the playfulness of the entity ended there. This was the source of the unholy stink, and the coffee urn wasn't the only metal object caught in its spinning current. Two more stacking chairs and a floor lamp spun around the ceiling as well, whirling so fast he could barely see them. The sight explained the chair that had broken the window—it had probably spun out of control like a crazy comet.

Time for action. Perry was nowhere in sight, but Alessandro wasn't about to wait any longer. He got two strides into the room before he sensed the entity take notice of him. It was like a brush of cold fingers as foul as its stink—as if something had reached from Alessandro's own abandoned grave to drag him back. He spun with a snarl, baring fangs, but there was no face, no form to confront.

All the same, the thing hurled the coffee urn. Alessandro ducked, his reflexes saving him. The urn smashed against the wall, punching a hole in the drywall and spraying scalding coffee throughout the room. The man on the floor howled in pain.

"Get up," Alessandro ordered.

"I *can't*," the man replied, his voice ragged with terror.

Wasting no more words, Alessandro grabbed him by the collar and dragged him to his feet, half-tossing him toward the relative safety of the others. Then he drew his sword, not because it would do him any good against whatever this was, but because it showed he meant business.

"What do you want?" he demanded of the mass of stinking sparkles.

"A white Christmas," it rasped with the withered whisper of the dead.

$\mathcal{A}$lessandro stood his ground, taking the thing's measure. The force of its attention tingled, as if its hostility carried an electric current. The vampire gripped his sword, considering the best way to smack the hellspawn back to the demon dimensions.

A moment later, Perry Baker ran into the room, carrying a duffel bag in one hand.

"Where were you?" Alessandro asked.

"Grabbing the emergency kit from the bus. I keep a few magical basics in it just in case, along with first aid supplies and a fire extinguisher. I never know what the seniors might get up to."

The werewolf set the bag down, hurrying over to stand beside him. Perry was lean and wiry, with wavy brown hair and a narrow, sensitive face. He jerked his chin toward the manifestation, his eyes flashing wolf-gold. "Thanks for coming. This thing threatened innocents."

Under normal circumstances, the old rogues in Pack Silvertail hardly qualified as innocents, but Alessandro nodded. "Our uninvited guest said it wants a white Christmas."

For a moment, they stood shoulder to shoulder, glowering at the sparkling mass. "Don't talk to it," Perry said softly. "Things like that try to get inside your head."

Alessandro cast him a sidelong look. "I'm familiar with demons."

"Yeah, but you usually arrest things with legs, not sparkly goo monsters."

"I'll be sure to put that on my resumé."

Perry frowned, ignoring his last remark. "Something about this hellspawn isn't normal."

"Such as?"

"It's singing."

Perry was right. The slime was crooning the famous Bing Crosby hit in a reedy, raspy voice. A moment later, a metal serving tray spun out of the whirlwind like a discus and clanged against the wall. The sudden movement made them both jump, the sword twitching in Alessandro's hand.

A murmur rose from the assembled seniors. Although the noise was soft, he could pick out a mix of fear and impatience that grated on Alessandro's already-frayed nerves.

"What's the plan?" he asked Perry.

"Did you bring the herbs?" The werewolf rubbed his hands together, then shook out his arms like an athlete about to show his stuff.

"Here you go." Without taking his eyes off the demon, Alessandro pulled the plastic bags from his pocket and handed them over.

A great glop of sparkling slime fell from the whirling mass, landing a few feet away. It seemed to pulse where it lay, like a malignant alien from a bad sci-fi flick.

"Great." After taking the herbs, Perry turned to address the huddled crowd. "Please, nobody touch the slime. Not to alarm you, but we don't know if it's safe."

"Whoa, listen to the boy genius!" called one of the wolves.

"This isn't my first hellspawn, son."

"Shut up, Bob," replied a female who might have been his mate. "He's just trying to help."

In truth, demon slime was usually toxic. That was just one of the many facts Alessandro wished he didn't need to know—and a worry if it decided to attack from above. He cleared his throat, raising his voice to be heard across the room. "What happens if you try to leave? I assume you've tried?"

"It stops us," Bob said. "It throws things."

"He's right. I ran outside to get the kit, but I'm faster," Perry muttered. "The elders are easy targets."

Alessandro calculated the distance between the seniors and the door, and then the force and speed of the serving tray that now lay crumpled on the floor. For an instant, he wished he were back in his cookie-scented kitchen reading the mail. "This started out as an average night."

"Get real." Perry shrugged. "Average isn't in our future. It's showtime."

"So true." Something inside Alessandro relaxed, and the predator side of his nature flowed in like the tide, filling countless corners of his soul. His softer side dropped away.

Perry returned to the duffel bag, then stooped to unzip it. The scent of incense floated up from the nylon bag, competing with the entity's stink. The werewolf grabbed a fistful of candles and arranged them on the floor along with Holly's herbs.

"Exorcism?" Alessandro asked.

"Banishment. That'll bench it for tonight at least."

Banishment was to exorcism like first aid was to surgery. It was quick and dirty, but it would do until they could bring in better tools and someone with more expertise.

Alessandro began sidestepping, moving just enough that the entity focused on him and not on Perry's preparations. Alessandro made an experimental lunge at the wall where the slime trickled in thick, glistening ropes. Chopping slime wasn't particularly effective, but the silver that coated his blade might be. Lots of unholy things hated its touch.

The trailing tentacle snapped back into the main blob with a squelch and an extra puff of stink. So it had excellent reflexes. Good to know.

Alessandro whirled as a loose pile of cutlery clattered upward from the coffee table and was sucked into the swirling mass. At the same moment, he felt a sharp tug on the sword. Was it using some sort of magnetic force to grab objects? With a snarl, he tightened his grip and slashed at another oozing trail, but it was too fast. In the next moment, all the trails of slime were slurped back into the main body and out of his reach. He heard a dry, wispy chuckle that rasped at his temper.

Then alarm hit him like a fist. Hazel Carver—Holly's grandmother—had shuffled forward from the other seniors, using two canes for support. By the time Alessandro noticed her, she was halfway to Perry's side.

"Hazel!" he snapped. "Stay back where it's safe."

Waving a hand in a gesture that might have been a greeting or a dismissal, she kept moving. Seething with frustration, Alessandro strode toward her. Her hair was pulled back in a long gray ponytail, showing off features that were still sharply defined. She wore a blue tunic and dark pants that said she'd dressed up to come out that night. Somehow, that detail made everything worse.

He gently put a hand on her shoulder, using just enough pressure to make her stop. "Please, get back."

A fork flew out of the whirling mass, quivering as it hit the doorframe and stuck. Grandma Carver ignored it, holding his gaze with eyes as bright a green as when he'd first met her. "I'm a Carver witch. I can withstand a bit of goop."

"It's dangerous."

She stared past him to Perry. "What exactly do you think you're doing?"

Perry glanced up, suddenly seeming very young. "Ma'am, please keep at a safe distance."

"Stuff and feathers," she said calmly. "You're using too much myrrh. We're banishing the demon, not embalming it. And add more henbane."

Alessandro dropped his hand, letting her pass. She had knowledge they needed. At the same time, he placed himself between her and the demon, blade at the ready. As if sensing trouble, the entity seemed to compress, shedding some of the debris caught in its cyclone. The last of the chairs shot toward Alessandro. He batted it aside, pain shooting up his left forearm as it clattered to the floor. Hot rage arrowed through him. If he'd been one of the seniors…no, he didn't have time to think about *what if.*

The entity shrank in circumference but streamed toward the floor in an extended column, re-absorbing the patch of glop that had fallen no more than a minute ago. Behind him, he heard the strike of a match, followed by the raw scent of burning sage. It was a clean and welcome relief from the peppermint grave stench.

More metal objects shot from the mass. Vampire-quick, Alessandro plucked a knife from the air and deflected a serving spoon with his blade. Somebody cried out from the back of the room, but he couldn't afford to turn and look.

On the positive side, there didn't seem to be any more solid objects whirling inside the entity. Less reassuring was that the column had changed, radiating a glow that quickly shifted from yellow to green to violet and back again, as if it couldn't decide its next move. He'd seen demons waver like this before. It was morphing between manifestations, which meant there was a tiny window for escape.

"Get out of here *now,*" Alessandro ordered, raising his voice so every one of the seniors could hear him. Stomach knotted by nerves, he poised to leap between the demon and its next victim.

"Go," Perry echoed, scrambling to help the seniors leave. Unruffled, Grandma Carver kept working on the spell circle Perry had cast. The tingle of rising power brushed against Alessandro's skin like a circling cat. This was the critical moment of a spell, as power rose and the ancient witch shaped it to her will. They couldn't afford a distraction.

Which meant Alessandro had to draw the demon's attention his way. He approached the column of light a step at a time, peering into it until his eyes watered. The colors were still shifting, but now there was the suggestion of a figure in its midst. It seemed to be a young man and then an old crone, a shaman and then a nurse, a businessman and then a soldier in fatigues. The kaleidoscope of features and garments was as chaotic as the whirlwind that had destroyed the room. Alessandro chanced a glance over his shoulder to see Perry leading the last of his charges through the door. Only Hazel Carver remained behind, protected within the circle she'd cast.

When he turned back, the shifting glow backlit a solid form. Before Alessandro could get a good look, a blade flashed through the air. The vampire twisted aside. The point raked his shoulder, leaving a lick of pain behind.

So it wanted to fight? Alessandro almost laughed. Now they were on familiar turf. He thrust his sword, aiming for the heart. The figure parried with a flick of its wrist, dancing away from harm. Cursing, Alessandro swiped downward in a blow that should have split the thing in two. Incredibly, his sword passed right through the demon. Alessandro stumbled, almost going to his knees. The thing was made of smoke.

The demon materialized and ripped the weapon from his hand. Alessandro recoiled, regaining his balance as the sword spun to the floor. He lunged toward it, but the figure blocked his path. Frustration made him curse, but he gave up on his blade for the moment. He was a vampire, and that made him a lethal weapon in his own right.

They circled like dogs. As they turned, he glimpsed Perry rejoining Grandma Carver at the spell circle. A white light gathered around it like enchanted mist. Alessandro had to keep the enemy occupied for just a little while longer. The figure kept shifting, one face to another, never settling into a single form. It was disturbing to watch.

But even as the thought formed, others chased it aside. The wreck of the seniors' social night depressed him. He thought of Hazel as a young woman, her wedding veil like lace made of glittering frost. He recalled the blanketing snows of his childhood, and the clear peal of the church bells over his mountain village.

A blow to his jaw snapped him back to the present. The fight wasn't on just a physical level—this thing had hypnotic powers something like a vampire's. It had nearly put him under. Furious, he pounced, claws and fangs extended. This time, he met something solid and bore it to the ground. The thing was strong, the limbs like steel. All the same, Alessandro managed to grasp its throat and squeeze.

His mother's eyes gazed into his own, their brimming sorrow an unexpected strike to his heart. It was a face he hadn't seen for the better part of seven centuries. For a split second of surprise, he dropped his guard. Just as fast, his mother was gone and the figure was his father, stinking of drink and rage. There were many kinds of demons, and this memory was one of Alessandro's worst.

His father's blow knocked him across the room—just like it had when he'd been a boy. Alessandro's skull rang as he hit the wall, the force holding him poised before he crumpled to his knees. Vision swimming, he raised his head to see the white mist from Hazel's spell drift upward. It bobbed and wavered before eventually forming a cloud on the ceiling.

The demon—still wearing the face of Alessandro's father—stalked toward him. Emotion thundered now, dragging more memories with it. Brothers and sisters huddled around the fire.

Hunger in the wintertime when the cold crept beneath the sheepskins that covered the straw mattress of his bed. Being sold to the nobleman who would eventually give him to the vampires.

Alessandro scrambled to his feet. "Stop wearing his face!"

His father spread his thick hands in a shrug. Beneath the drink-coarsened features was the young man he'd been before the plague had taken his wife—Alessandro's mother—along with half the village. The loss had broken their family apart.

The sight tore something in Alessandro's heart, and a cry, or a curse, choked him. Out of desperation, he jerked his gaze away. His eyes caught the cloud. It appeared harmless, but it rested in the exact spot where the whirlwind had been. There, the mist Hazel had raised dissolved into a perfect circle of darkness, as if someone had torn a hole in reality.

His attention flicked back to his father. He was gone, replaced by a twisting column of sparkling light. Slowly, as if struggling against an unseen force, the light broke apart into strands of sparkling mist. Then it drifted into the darkness as if sucked out by a powerful fan. A raw keening filled the room as bit by bit, it swirled upward.

Alessandro sagged in relief as, eventually, both the noise and the stink dissipated. The demon had roused long-forgotten pain, and he immediately wondered how much his companions had seen. Vampires never shared their human past with others.

He needn't have worried. Hazel Carver leaned on Perry's arm with a smile on her lips, clearly pleased that she'd won. Perry hung his head as if exhausted. "I don't think the spell is going to last. That thing is strong."

"Did you learn anything about it?" Alessandro asked, working hard to keep his voice steady. The creature had violated him. A literal demon had reached inside and pulled out the private demons from his past. He ran his hands down his chest as if expecting to find a gaping tear.

"Not a lot," Perry said. "I don't know for sure, but I don't think this is the first time it's shown up. There was a small disturbance a week ago at a retro movie theater. Then a vintage craft fair across the street."

"Those were the same entity," Hazel said, her tone flat. "The behavior is too similar to be anything else."

"Why is this the first time I'm hearing about it?"

"Probably because those incidents weren't nearly so spectacular," Perry replied. "Plus, there's always something weird going on in this neighborhood. Maybe it just didn't seem worth bothering about."

"Isn't the theater showing old Christmas films right now?" Alessandro asked, turning to Hazel.

"Yes," she said. "Old holiday memories seem to be this demon's favorite theme."

Perry was packing up the extra magical supplies, leaving the spell circle in place. "I've never heard of a nostalgic demon. Or would that be demonic nostalgia?"

"You'd be surprised," the old witch answered. "Were you at the movies when the demon showed itself?"

"Yes."

"Who were you with?"

"Just a date," Perry said evasively. "Does it matter?"

"The right lover is never *just* anything. If the demon responds to emotion, clearly you weren't the one summoning it there."

Perry's ears turned pink. "Probably not."

Hazel rolled her eyes. "Then stop wasting your time like a clueless pup. At this point in your life, you should be making memories sweet enough to have this demon drooling."

Alessandro tuned out the conversation, lost again in the memory of his family. Were those recollections of his parents real? How much of his long life did he remember clearly, and how much had he rewritten over the years?

Perry rose, clearly done with Hazel's opinions on his love life. "I really need to get my seniors home."

Alessandro retrieved his sword and joined the wolf as he walked to the door, Hazel moving slowly between them. "Were there any injuries?" the vampire asked.

"Just some bruising," Perry said. "Bob got hit with a flying spoon, but he'll be fine. Thanks for coming when I called."

"Always." Alessandro squeezed his shoulder in farewell.

Perry herded his charges onto the bus while the employee who had been running the bingo night called taxis for the remaining guests. The man was rattled but otherwise fine. Still, Alessandro lingered while he locked up the center for the night, just in case.

Hazel waited patiently on a bench by the door, a bundle on her lap. Setting it aside, she rose when Alessandro came toward her. "How are you doing now that the excitement is over?" she asked.

"I was about to ask you the same thing," he replied.

"I wasn't the one exchanging blows."

They'd managed to dodge one another's questions. Alessandro knew she wasn't likely to give in first. "I'm fine," he finally said. "I wouldn't recommend the experience, though."

"I'm not surprised that manifestation visited a group of old fogies," she said, pulling out a gold cigarette case. She was a chain smoker, but after so many years, Alessandro had given up lecturing. He pulled out his own lighter—yeah, he smoked but he was already dead—and waited as she inhaled and blew out a perfect series of rings.

"What do you mean?" he asked once the last ring had drifted away.

"Our demon visitor is summoned by emotions, memories, or both," she said. "Maybe it's fueled by them, too. Either way, it's only going to get more dangerous as we get closer to the holidays."

"Why is it here in Fairview?" He pulled out his car keys, ready to drive her home.

"I'm not sure, but we only put a bandage on the problem tonight. When it returns, and it will, watch out."

"Why?"

"We've made it mad." She smiled, a network of wrinkles creasing her apple cheeks. "Besides, if it's fueled by our thoughts and emotions, it's a volatile time of year. Christmas isn't all eggnog and mistletoe, dearest. Or hadn't you noticed that?"

She was baiting him, but he let it go. It was just her way of keeping distance between herself and a vampire, however much they were friends.

"How worried should I be?" he asked.

She held his gaze. "Tell Holly to schedule a proper exorcism for tomorrow."

ALESSANDRO DROPPED Hazel at the door of the Golden Swans, the supervised care facility where she lived. He offered to walk her upstairs, but she declined. It was one thing to have a young man escort her to the door in hopes of a kiss, but quite another to be watched for signs of impending collapse. She'd keep her dignity as long as possible, thank you very much.

Once inside the heavy glass doors, she took the elevator up to her floor. It was a nice residence, convenient and clean. She had her own apartment and as much or as little nursing care as she needed. The only drawback was leaving the old Carver house, where she'd grown up, married, and raised children of her own. There, too, she'd raised her granddaughters after their parents had died. But once Holly and Ashe were adults, it had been time to let go of the old place and its many flights of stairs. Her knees and hips had thanked her, even if her heart still ached a bit.

It had been for the best. Now the girls were raising families of their own, and the Carver name would be passed from mother to daughter for another generation. The house would be full come Yuletide, and she'd join in the songs and food and spoil her great-grandchildren as much as their parents would allow. That was how things were meant to be.

She unlocked the door to her apartment and went inside, catching the scent of the flowers Ashe, her eldest granddaughter, had brought by that morning. The white lilies and red chrysanthemums were a perfect early Yuletide gift, especially when they came with a tray of homemade brownies. Hazel had worried about Ashe for a long time, but the girl seemed to be turning out all right.

Hazel went to the dining room—which was really an extension of the tiny living room—and set down the bundle she'd brought from the community center. Relieved of her burden, she made tea, turned on the gas fireplace, and sat down to think.

She'd wrapped the bundle in her headscarf. Now she unwound the cloth and set it aside. The holiday cards had been tied up with string, but it was old and broke after a light tug. The stack of thin cardboard slumped into an uneven pile, shedding glitter onto the tablecloth. Hazel picked up the top one—Victorian kittens sledding down a snowy hill—and opened it to see the greeting.

"To Hazel from Tom," she read aloud, feeling a rush of affection as she said her husband's name. This had been the first card he'd given her so many Decembers ago. They hadn't even been engaged yet.

And she'd nearly lost these cards—the only things he'd ever written to her, since they had almost never been apart. Swallowing hard, she cursed her carelessness. She'd donated some of her holiday decorations to the community center and the cards had been hiding in the bottom of the box—possibly packed there during her move from the Carver house. An awful oversight. She'd never voluntarily give these away.

Perry's aunt Margaret had been the member of the decorating committee to find the bundle and set it aside, rightly assuming Hazel would want them back. There were well over fifty years of greetings, enough to cover courtship to their golden anniversary and beyond—right up until Tom's final year. Always sentimental, Margaret had cried over the forgotten cache of memories, nearly taking Hazel down with her.

The manifestation had shown up immediately after that, sucking up the cards before it absorbed everything else into its whirlwind. That was a clue about its nature. Each time it had shown up—at the movie theater, the vintage fair, and tonight—the air was charged with holiday-related memories. As she'd explained to Alessandro, objects that triggered emotions could be conduits to certain kinds of demonic energy, almost the way a power outlet accessed electricity. The creature must have sniffed out their sentimental power, then used them as a door into the mortal world.

She lit another cigarette, thinking about Alessandro's expression after the demon had left. Whatever he'd experienced—some past memory, no doubt—had left him raw. Even the Undead couldn't escape their pasts. Or maybe, *especially* the Undead. They didn't have the luxury of oblivion.

Hazel gathered the cards into a stack. They'd been on the carpet after the creature had fled, dropped when it had taken a human form to fight Alessandro. She would have to thank the vampire properly for giving her Tom's words back. Her husband might be gone, but he still ruled her heart.

A witch had two paths—to extend her life indefinitely through magic, like Holly, or to age and die naturally, like Ashe and Hazel herself. A witch's lifespan was a few decades longer than a human's, but she had opted to join Tom rather than face an eternity without him.

Memories. She released a puff of smoke, her magic shaping it into familiar, dear features that hovered close enough to kiss. *Tom.* She could almost feel the soft warm pressure of lips, the gust of his breath on her cheek, but then the air currents broke the image apart. She watched them go, eyes dry but with a choking pain in her throat.

Why, with all the ghosts that haunted Fairview, had her Tom never come back to her?

CHAPTER 3

HAZEL'S STORY

ecember 1945

HAZEL CARVER WORKED at the wooden table in the kitchen of the family home. She'd turned it into her unofficial desk despite the many rooms upstairs—the kitchen was the heart of the place, warm from the oven and smelling of gingerbread and yeast. Today, she was writing Yule cards to family, friends, and supernatural allies all over the country. The postage took a bite from the household budget, but it was wise to keep networks fresh. Besides, sending cards was a mark of good manners. It might be a brave new world now that the war was over, but a bit of polish still mattered.

She hummed along with Judy Garland as the chanteuse wished everyone a merry little Christmas. The Westinghouse radio had been a free gift that came with the new refrigerator, which they'd just managed to pay off. It had been an extravagance, but Rose, her older sister, had insisted they keep up with the times. Appearances mattered to Rose. Keeping the family solvent mattered to Hazel.

New appliances meant Hazel had to work twice as hard to make ends meet. Good penmanship had made her the correspondence clerk for the Carver family and for the Three Sisters Agency, the witchcraft business handed down from mothers to daughters since the 1880s. She was also the one who paid the bills and chased down clients who owed them money—although they'd take eggs or milk or anything worth trading. Times had been uncertain ever since she'd been a little girl.

The thunka-thunk of a treadle sewing machine rumbled through the hardwood floors. Rose was sewing their Yule presents, which meant she wouldn't let anyone inside the room. Their cousin, Phyllis, was downtown leading a seance at the Empire Hotel, with all its fine china and beautiful crystal. All through the war, the bereaved yearned to know their dead slept peacefully. The wealthy patrons of the Empire were no different, and Phyllis was the best at what she did.

Feeling enormously efficient, Hazel sealed the envelope of the card she'd just written and addressed it, setting it on the neat pile of finished correspondence to her left. Then she picked up a fresh card from the box to her right, opened it to write her greeting, and paused, the nib of her fountain pen poised in the air.

This one would be to Ashton, her older brother. He had come home from the war, but like so many others, he hadn't been able to settle down. Most recently, he'd moved to Chicago, but Hazel doubted that would last. He'd been recruited into the band of witches who'd foiled the German bombers over England—one of the most powerful magical workings of the modern age. Rose said he'd come back shell-shocked. If that were true, there was even more reason for her brother to come home.

She set down her pen, a burn of resentment in her breast. What right did he have to turn his back on their family? They could use his help to put food on the table, but Hazel wanted his guidance even more. Now that their parents were gone, they had to find their way alone.

She started to write, then glowered at Ashton's name. Some things just shouldn't change, brave new world or not. Hazel gave up on wishing him a Happy Yule, at least until her temper cooled.

The sharp rap of the brass knocker interrupted her annoyance. After screwing the cap on her pen, she rose to answer, switching the radio off on the way. It might be a client with ready cash to spend, so she smoothed the creases from her skirt and checked the seams of her stockings. Then, with a deep breath, she opened the heavy door. A young man stood on the steps, his hat in his hand and a hopeful expression in his blue eyes.

Instinct said he wasn't there to spend money. Disappointment twisted in her chest even as those blue eyes made her a little dizzy. "Good afternoon."

"Hello, miss."

"Is there something I can do for you?"

A confident smile spread over his face. He was about Ashton's age, handsome and fair-haired. "It's more like what can I do for you?"

"Excuse me?"

His expression turned hopeful and a little desperate. "Surely there's something that needs fixing?"

Hazel raised an eyebrow. The houses that belonged to old witch families like the Carvers maintained themselves. They never needed paint or repairs, or even much cleaning for that matter, and the yards were almost as good. This young man—clearly a mere human—couldn't be from around here or he would know that.

"I'm Tom Turner," he offered.

He was just another soldier back from the war, searching for work in this scarce market. He wasn't part of her world. The best thing she could do was shoo him off the porch, yet she was curious. This was the kind of man Ashton had met during the war. What was it he saw that made him live among humans now?

She studied Tom Turner, using a touch of her magic. "You were in the Air Force?"

His eyes widened in surprise, but he nodded. "Yes, Miss Carver."

It was her turn to be startled. "How did you know my name?"

"I saw you in town and asked who you were," he said, acting as if that was the most normal thing in the world. Maybe it was when a person had no magic.

"Do you know what kind of business we run here?" she asked.

He grinned, his confidence secure once more. "Sure. I didn't figure there would be too many with the gumption to knock on a witch's door, so I got here first. Do you have any odd jobs I could do?"

Annoyance flashed through her. He was so certain she was harmless. "And you're not concerned that all those people afraid of knocking on my door have the right idea?"

For the first time, he lowered those amazing blue eyes. She felt the loss of his gaze like the sun ducking beyond a cloud. It was then, when she wasn't dazzled, that she saw he was hungry, tired, and out of ideas. There were veterans just like him all over, released from service and unsure of their futures. The G.I. Bill offered a helping hand to returning soldiers, but it wasn't a magic wand.

This encounter was beyond the boundaries of her comfort, but she couldn't bring herself to turn him away. Nerves humming through her bones, Hazel pushed open the door. Tom Turner was clearly human and had no business in the Carver house, but he needed someone to be decent to him. In a world gone mad, that was one thing Hazel could control.

"Come inside," she said, her voice sounding strange in her own ears.

Tom did as she asked, climbing the porch stairs slowly while favoring his right leg. Hazel wondered if he'd been wounded, but was too shy to ask. Then he wiped his feet on the welcome mat like someone whose mother had strong opinions on mud. As Hazel led him inside, she heard the house whisper to itself, considering the newcomer.

"You see?" she said lightly. "The house is in good repair."

Of course, the furnishings were a little shabby, but she only noticed that when they had guests. And there was a quality about him, a way he had of being fully present, that made his focus just a little overwhelming. Her cheeks heated as he scanned the room.

"You have a very pleasant home," he said politely.

The comment did nothing to dispel the strange feeling of intimacy, as if showing him the parlor was the same as granting him a peek at her garters. His attention fell on the cat bed, sitting empty next to the sofa. "Oh," she said softly. "That belonged to our cat, Grimm. He passed away last week, and I haven't had the heart to put his bed away." That was another loss, different from losing Ashton, but in its own way just as sharp.

"I'm sorry, miss," Tom said. "It's always a sad thing when a friend leaves us."

He'd said *friend*, not pet or animal. It was a slight thing, but she couldn't help but notice. There was at least one subject where they understood one another. Still, she let the matter drop. The last thing she wanted was a conversation with a stranger about something that still hurt so badly.

She led him through to the kitchen, then waved him to a seat at the wooden table. Quickly, she shuffled her writing materials aside. "You're doing your Christmas cards," he remarked. "I apologize for interrupting you."

"I was ready for a break," she said, not bothering to explain that witches celebrated Yule instead. She was glad to have a new topic of conversation. "Writing them takes a while, but it's worth doing. It's the only time I keep in touch with some people. Would you like something to eat?"

The question seemed to take him off guard. He seemed as if he would refuse, but she could tell he wanted to accept. Without waiting for him to answer, she bustled to the counter and took a loaf from the bread box. It was a day old, so she released a slight spell to ensure it tasted fresh.

"I just have cheese and cucumbers for sandwiches," she said, slicing the bread. "We ate the last of the Sunday roast last night."

He swallowed hard. "I'm grateful for your kindness."

From there, the strangeness between them melted. While he ate and she made tea, they talked. He was from Portland, had never met a witch before, and had a sister named May. He'd been shot down, but landed in friendly territory. She also heard about his job search. He'd signed up to serve right out of school, and he wanted to keep working around planes.

"What services does the Three Sisters Agency offer?" he asked.

"Mostly, we are hired to help ghosts move on. We help their surviving loved ones move on as well, in a way. My cousin, Phyllis, is very good at contacting the dead."

Tom frowned. "That doesn't sound very cheerful."

"Depends on the ghost." Hazel shrugged. "Rose also does some fortune-telling. If something more serious ever comes up, sometimes we can help." She didn't mention the vampires or the minor demon they'd wrestled. Some things one just didn't tell a blue-eyed stranger straight off the bat.

"Do you sell love potions?" Tom asked with a sly smile.

"Those are always more trouble than they're worth."

"Don't they make money?"

"Sure, but some magic makes you pay in other ways."

"Ah." He sobered. "So how is business?"

"Slow," she said. "They say things will pick up, with all kinds of new industry, but I'm still waiting."

Tom ate the last of his sandwich, nodding a little as if she'd only confirmed his suspicions. "Well then, I suppose I should take my search for a job elsewhere."

Hazel shook her head, genuinely sorry. "We don't make enough money to hire anybody, even if there was a chore we needed done."

"I'm sure there's something I can do in return for lunch."

"It was just a sandwich," she protested, her cheeks flaring with heat.

He picked up a stack of handbills that sat next to the cards she'd been writing. "What are you going to do with these?"

"Put them up in shop windows." The notices were simple, giving the agency's name and address and reminding the townsfolk of their services. They had been Hazel's idea to drum up business.

"How about I deliver these for you?" he asked. "I'll be heading around town anyway."

"Are you sure you want to?" she asked, casting a quick glance at his leg. "Walking can't be that comfortable."

"It's no trouble, miss," Tom said with his signature slow smile.

"Still…"

"No job is too small, especially if it's paid for in kindness."

She'd run out of protests. Hazel let him take the handbills and showed him to the door, thanking him for doing her this favor. She was honestly grateful. If he hadn't come along, she would have been the one to do it.

It certainly wouldn't have been Rose. In fact, Hazel waited a few days before telling her sister about Tom.

"You invited a human into our house?" Rose asked, turning her head from side to side as she gazed into her dressing table mirror. She was trying a new hairstyle, copied from the latest human fashion magazine. The irony of it was apparently quite lost on her.

Hazel came up behind her sister, fixing the hairpins where Rose couldn't reach. Rose's hair was a sunlit gold, unlike Hazel's dull brown, but it was fine and slippery. Hazel began working in a bit of magic to make the pins hold.

"He was nice," Hazel said.

"So is a stray puppy. That doesn't mean you have to adopt one."

"He's putting up our notices."

"You could've given the paperboy an extra fifty cents to do it. You didn't have to invite a stranger to lunch."

"It wasn't like that."

"Then how was it?"

Uncomfortable, Hazel thought, but that didn't excuse Rose's attitude. She accidentally on purpose stabbed her with a pin.

"*Ow,*" Rose squeaked.

"Sorry." Hazel almost meant it.

"Just keep your priorities straight," her sister said stiffly. "I did, and look where I'm headed."

Next June, Rose would be marrying into an important family from Baltimore—witches whose bloodline went back a thousand years. The marriage been arranged by the Elders to keep the magical dynasty strong.

"Don't you mind it?" Hazel asked softly.

"That's the way things have always been done," Rose answered, her jaw set. Still, Hazel saw the shadows in her eyes.

"That doesn't make it right," Hazel said. The war had made her think differently about words like *purity* and *bloodline*.

"The Elders will find a husband for you, too, if you ask."

On some level, Hazel had planned for just that, but she realized she'd changed her mind. Emphatically. "Times are changing."

Hazel put in the last pin, then stepped back from Rose's chair. Her sister explored the updo with tentative fingers. "Maybe you're the one who's changing," Rose said. "Just like Ashton."

"Don't be ridiculous," Hazel snapped. "I'm not like him at all. I want the Three Sisters to keep going. I want our way of life to survive."

"Maybe it can't. Not if we all leave. The times are changing, you know." Rose's smug smile said she was deliberately needling her.

Hazel left the room.

She needed air. It felt as if the Carver house was crumbling from its foundations. Grabbing up her coat and gloves, she almost ran out the front door, deciding to head for town. It was only midafternoon, though dusk was already creeping into the sky. The temperature was cold enough for frost to sparkle on the fence posts. Hazel walked quickly, her breath coming in gusts of steam.

As she approached town, she noticed new strings of electrical Christmas lights. Celluloid reindeer pranced in the windows beneath aluminum icicles. The effect was bright, but felt too new. She preferred natural pine boughs and real mistletoe. Electric lights weren't nearly as pretty on a tree as real candles.

She wasn't changing; that wasn't it at all. Everything else— even the decorations—was pushing her outside the comfortable world she'd always known. The time of year—soaked in tradition and family ideals—just highlighted the tension.

Hazel found a public telephone and stepped inside the booth, closing the door behind her. She fished coins from her purse, her fingers clumsy with cold, and gave Ashton's Chicago number to the operator. They had a telephone at the house, but this wasn't a call she wanted Rose or Phyllis to overhear.

It took forever to connect, but whether that was normal, she couldn't say. The only other long-distance calls she'd made had been when her father died years ago. Eventually, after a lot of clicks and pops and static sounds, Ashton came on the line.

"Hazel? What's wrong?" His voice sounded strained, as if he could barely hear her.

Hazel spoke up. "Nothing's wrong."

"Then why did you call?"

It was a good question. So many things crowded her—how

she would keep the agency going when Rose left, and whether Rose would be happy in her marriage. She needed to know why Ashton had left, and if he was as confused as she was. Was there even a place for witches in this new age of progress? Were the old ways still right?

She felt vulnerable then, sorely in need of reassurance. Phyllis was fifteen years older and settled in her ways. Rose had problems of her own. But Ashton was her big brother. Surely he had advice.

The need to talk ached in her throat, but the crackling, popping line only underscored the distance between them. The notion of shouting her insecurities so he could hear them on the other end made her cringe. She needed to see his face as she bared her soul.

"Are you coming home for Yule?" she asked instead. Maybe she was hanging onto an old life she couldn't keep, but she would feel so much better with her family gathered around the table for a holiday celebration. Then they could talk. "Please say you are."

"No," Ashton replied. "No, I'm not coming back. Maybe not for a long time."

I need you. But she couldn't say it so bluntly. Not with the operator right there. "It's not a family holiday without you."

"You'll learn to do without me," he replied. "That's just how it has to be."

"But why?" Hazel's voice held a note of desperation. Now she remembered she'd been mad at him, mad to the point she didn't want to send a card.

"It's not the same now," Ashton said gently. "I have a life here. A good one with ordinary people. After what I saw overseas, this is what I need right now. Please, Hazel, try to understand."

"They aren't your people."

"They are now. Us. Them. It's meaningless. Things aren't as cut and dried as you might think. The world is a bigger place than I knew."

Maybe it *was* that simple. His world had grown, and now he was inhabiting a different part of it. One where he'd found peace and she didn't belong.

A coldness that had nothing to do with December flooded through her. She hung up the phone without saying goodbye. Ashton wasn't going to help her—not with the agency, the family, or anything at all. He was gone. Rose was going. The cozy, family-centered vision Hazel had held for the future was drifting apart like mist, and the future didn't look anything like what she'd expected.

She got halfway home before the scalding tears began. When they said Yule was the darkest time of the year, they were right.

And yet, the days marched on. Just before the solstice, a neighbor brought them a Yule tree. Hazel put it in a stand, securing it with a spell, and began to decorate despite her black mood. She was still wrestling with her conversation—or lack of it —with her brother. As the youngest, she was used to her family filling up her world with their plans and ideas. What Hazel had never counted on was finding her future a blank canvas awaiting choices of her own.

She could marry. She could try to keep the agency running. She could begin to explore magic much larger than the domestic spells that were her usual stock-in-trade. Or she could do none of those things. The terror and the glory of those decisions were hers alone.

Alone. The word said it all. Even tonight, Rose was at a dance and Phyllis had gone to visit friends. Hazel was home alone on the night when family tradition said they should gather together to trim the tree. When a knock came at the door, she was grateful for the distraction.

It was Tom, his smile telling her that he was half afraid she would send him away—and yet, equally and irritatingly confident that she would invite him in. He was holding his muffler bundled around a coal-black kitten no bigger than his hand.

Hazel felt herself melting where she stood.

"This little boy came from the farm where I'm staying just out of town," Tom said. "The family is keeping the others, but they didn't want the black one. I thought he might find a welcome here."

Human or not, here was a handsome veteran bearing an adorable kitten. Hazel opened the door. "Come in. All I have is herb tea. Not everybody likes it, I'm afraid."

Tom came up the steps, that grin still playing around his mouth. "I can learn to like an awful lot. I figure I won't know until I try."

"You have all the right answers, don't you?"

His expression turned rueful. "I went through a lot of wrong ones first."

There was a story there—one Hazel wanted to hear. She put the kettle on before joining Tom in the parlor, where he'd set the scarf with its kitten filling on the floor.

"I didn't realize witches had Christmas trees," he said.

"Just about everybody believes in celebrating love and light at the turning of the year." She thought of Ashton, finding peace far away. Maybe he was right, and things weren't as cut and dried as she'd once thought. "People are more the same than they are different."

"I hope the Powers That Be remember that the next time they start a war."

Bitterness filled his voice, but not as much as she guessed he had a right to. All the same, Hazel was suddenly tongue-tied, wondering what tragedies he'd seen. She was saved when the kitten, finally warmed enough to escape the scarf, began batting the ornaments on the lowest branches of the tree. She dove to pick the little bundle up, marveling at the round belly beneath the soft cloud of fur. "Aren't you a pretty boy? And a naughty one."

The kitten blinked at her, the picture of innocence. With

some misgivings, she set it down again and it scampered off, tail held high.

Tom picked that moment to hand her three of the handbills he'd been putting up around town. When she turned them over, she saw names and telephone numbers scribbled on the back. "What's this?"

"You have some appointments," he said. "I had a few conversations as I was delivering your advertising around town."

There were only three appointments, but Hazel knew how gossip spread in a small town. Three might be all she needed to start boosting the agency's clientele. Just the way Tom understood animals were friends, he knew the agency mattered to her. "I'm more grateful than I can say."

She reached out, and that was the first time she felt the rough warmth of Tom Turner's hand. Her mouth went suddenly dry, a flutter stirring deep in her belly.

"Then say you'll let me take you to dinner." His blue eyes were bright and as full of mischief as the little cat's. "I've landed a job at the airfield. It's a small commercial business, but it's what I want."

"How did that come about?" She let go of his fingers, forcing herself to remember she was a proper young lady. She'd already broken a thousand rules by asking him in when she was alone in the house.

"Chance," Tom replied. "When I went into a diner to leave one of your handbills, I overheard a conversation between the owner and his friend. They're looking to expand. I know how to keep books as well as fix planes. The company is getting two men for the price of one."

The kitten, caring nothing about jobs or planes, decided it was time to climb the tree. Hazel squeaked with dismay, lunging forward to pluck it from the branches. Tom reached out at the same time, and they ended up face to face with the fuzzy menace between them. She couldn't have engineered a more perfect moment using all the spell books in the Carver library. Sometimes, magic just happened.

"Oh dear," she whispered. His breath fanned her face. She was petrified, afraid to lean in and terrified to pull away. Tom solved the problem by making the first move. His kiss was as warm as the rest of him, gentle but firm in a way that set her entire body humming.

"Will you let me take you to dinner tonight?" he asked again.

The question was so simple, yet it covered such a vast territory. If the future *was* awaiting her design, did she want Tom in it? She suddenly understood Ashton and his talk of complexities. And yet, some things weren't difficult at all. In that moment, Hazel had her answer.

"I was planning on writing a card to my brother, but I think he'll understand if it's a day late. Nothing ever goes the way we think it will. Especially not during the holidays."

resent Day

HAZEL WOKE FROM HER REVERIE, the memory so close she could almost touch it. She wiped the tears from her cheeks with the cuff of her sweater. They weren't sorrowful tears, nor even joyful ones, but the overflow of a full life filled with both. She'd married Tom the next summer, and they'd stayed together for nearly sixty years—and she'd join him soon enough. No, none of it was what she'd expected when she'd opened the door that December morning to find him waiting on her doorstep like a stray.

Some people—like Rose—had questioned her marriage to a human, but Tom had encouraged her to become the witch she was, powerful and as deeply educated in the craft as anyone in her generation. Rather than hold her back, he'd pushed her to fulfill her gifts.

Ashton, of course, hadn't uttered a word of protest. In the end, he and Tom had become good friends. Though an outsider, Tom had knitted her family back together again. And then they'd had children of their own—and then came grandchildren, and great-grandchildren.

Hazel took a sip of her tea, found it cold, and went to the sideboard for her decanter of brandy. She'd earned a nightcap.

The astringent scent cleared her head when she lifted the snifter. In that moment, she sensed a flickering echo of the demon from the community hall. They had banished it, but it was feeling for cracks between the worlds, like a child with a puzzle box. If it found the smallest chink, it would tear its way back into this world—and then come hunting for those who had cast it out.

Memories and Christmas. Her reverie had all but offered it an open window, and the trigger for those dreams had been her stash of cards. The creature had used them as an entry point once before, and it could easily use them again. Demons were like metaphysical slugs, leaving a trail of their own substance behind them.

Hazel set the brandy down and shuffled to the kitchen, returning with a large, round canister of salt. She swiped a hand over the stack of cards, spreading them out, and began salting them with generous shakes of the container. It was messy, but she'd get one of her granddaughters to vacuum up the mess later.

She'd barely covered a third of the cards when they began to sizzle and smoke, giving off the same nauseating stench of peppermint and grave dirt. Slowly straightening, Hazel felt the unmistakable creep of gooseflesh as something lurked behind her. She froze, all too aware she was in no condition to run, and she'd left her purse with her phone in the other room. Animal fear rocked her for an instant, pain flaring in her chest before she slammed her self-control back into place. Her best weapons were experience and guile. Good thing she had a lot of both.

Hazel peered over her shoulder. The figure standing in the far hall was shadowy, not yet formed with any detail. That didn't mean it was weak. It took enormous power to cross the walls of space and time—more than she wanted to fight twice in one evening. She would have to work fast to save herself.

Hazel ripped the top from the salt canister, upending it over the cards. They bubbled and hissed, fogging the air with smoke and stink. Then she swept the whole mess together, grabbing the scarf she'd set aside to bundle the pile into her arms. She started for the fireplace. The last thing she wanted to do was burn Tom's precious words, but he'd forgive her.

She made it halfway across the room before the figure from the hallway approached. Hazel's feet failed her, refusing to move. Somehow, the demon had caught her thoughts, and now it was Tom walking toward her—young and sure, his face unlined and his shoulders broad with muscle. Her breath caught, an emotion as bright and fine as a butterfly's wing fluttering for one glorious second before reason stilled it.

"You forgot the limp," Hazel said to the thing wearing Tom's face. "He never quite lost it."

The corner of its mouth went down into a semi-frown, just the way she recalled. The demon was a good mimic. Anger twisted in her chest, hot as a flame. Fine—anger was better than fear.

"Didn't you miss me?" it asked.

Her heart wrenched, nearly making her cry out. She missed everything—the half-finished crosswords and horrible cigars, his fishing expeditions, and the way he still held her hand at the movies, even when they were as old as dirt. "I miss *him*," she said, taking a step back to put distance between herself and the demon.

"Especially this time of year," Tom said. "This is the anniversary of our kiss."

Rage shot through her. That wasn't Tom's smile, but something serpentine.

The creature reached out, cold fingers brushing her hand. The chill of the grave rushed up her spine, as cold as if she'd reached into her freezer. She took three unsteady steps toward the fire, suddenly desperate for its warmth.

"Hazel," it said. "All I want is your love."

Love. Memories. Emotions. All the things that made the holidays bright—or dark. It fed on their energy.

When she dropped to her knees, her eyes streamed with the pain of hitting the floor. She fumbled with the fire screen, the hot metal biting her fingers without mercy.

Its hand fell on her shoulder. It might have picked her up and hurled her through the wall, or over the balcony to smash on the street below. It wouldn't take much to kill her—but that would gain the demon nothing. The things it wanted could never come from the dead.

Cold soaked into her, gathering inside and filling her up like snow in a valley. Consciousness fell away, shrinking back to a distant pinpoint in a vastness of space. Hazel's fingers stilled, suspended in space. Emotions snuffed out one by one—guilt, curiosity, even fright. The demon took them all, gorging on her strength even as she struggled. She squeezed her eyes tight, straining to summon her magic, but it slipped away like a half-remembered dream. Only the hot coals of her anger remained.

"Give me the cards," the demon whispered in Tom's voice. "You don't need them anymore."

Hazel opened her eyes. She'd forgotten the bundle in her lap, mixed with the salt no demon could abide. *Fool,* she thought, not sure which of them she meant. The cards were its gateway into the world now, a path it had traveled with success. Naturally, it wanted them back for safekeeping.

And once it was in the mortal realm, it could feed on every soul, stirring up the embers of thrills and heartbreaks, long-forgotten feuds, and the sweet, private moments never meant to be shared. Evidently, the holiday flavors were its preferred meal.

Hazel wasn't sure what would be left after it gorged. Would there be nothing but a gulf in their memories where those memories should have been? That wasn't a risk she was willing to take. The cards were just paper, but her past was part of her soul.

She thrust the bundle into the fire with a savage shriek of rage. The sound jerked her back to full awareness. Magic slipped into her hands like a familiar pistol grip, and she made the fire flare, burning the remnants of the demon's gateway to ash.

She might be old, but she was still a Carver witch. It would take more than some would-be Krampus to put her down.

"WHAT DO YOU MEAN, Grandma tried to burn down the seniors' residence?" Holly asked Alessandro an hour later, when he'd barely got through the door.

It was getting close to dawn, and Alessandro was weary. He'd stopped to check in on the community center one last time when he'd received the call from the Golden Swans. "That's not quite what happened. She set off the fire alarm, that's all."

"What did she do? She didn't fall asleep smoking, did she?"

"No. Apparently the demon followed her home and appeared as your grandfather." Alessandro finished shedding his coat and boots, then put an arm around his partner's slender waist. Holly was in her bathrobe now, ready to go to bed as the dawn approached. They walked back to the kitchen, talking quietly as they went so as not to wake Robin. The little girl had finally nodded off in the downstairs bedroom, but she was a notoriously light sleeper.

When he finished repeating what Hazel had told him about the demon's visit, Holly's expression was thunderous. "You bet I'm going to exorcise its ass first thing tomorrow. I'll go in daylight when it will be weaker."

Which meant Alessandro wouldn't be there. "Take Ashe. She'll be every bit as furious as we are by what happened."

However else he felt about his vampire-slaying sister-in-law, Alessandro knew she'd fight to the death for Holly. Although she'd lost her magic, Ashe was as lethal as any monster. She was the best daylight substitute for his own protection.

"Okay." Holly seemed to sink into her own thoughts. "Why did it come back as Grandpa Tom?"

For the same reason it had appeared as his parents, he guessed. "Her memory of him is powerful."

"That's horrible. Grandma adored him. She should never have had to face something like that."

"No one should." He wondered what else the thing might dig out of his lengthy existence. The winter he'd spent in the court of Henry Tudor? The night he had danced the pavane with Anne Boleyn? Or the many years he'd spent as the vampire queen's executioner? There were plenty of gaudy horrors to choose from, yet the demon had retrieved echoes of a human life long lost to the shadows of time. There was a lot to ponder.

But as a parent, he didn't have the luxury of holding onto his thoughts for long.

"Paaaa!" Robin crowed as she lurched down the hallway, using the wall for support. The blanket she dragged with her puddled around her feet, tripping her so she plopped down hard.

Alessandro spotted the trembling lower lip and warded off the coming tears by scooping up child and blanket. "What are you doing out of bed?"

By way of reply, Robin fell against his shoulder, closing her eyes and putting her thumb—and a quantity of blanket fringe— into her mouth. Holly came to join them where they stood in the doorway between the kitchen and living room, where decorations were up and waiting for the big day.

"The tree does take up a lot of room," she observed.

It was a complete change of topic, but he didn't mind. He'd had enough gloom for one night. "I believe the principle of Christmas trees is to go big or go home."

"Apparently." They'd put up the gigantic fir a few days ago. It shimmered with tinsel, a gleaming ghost in the dark room. A few sturdier presents sat under the boughs for show, while the rest were stowed away safe from little fingers.

"It's been a long time since there was a proper Yule celebration in this house," Holly said. "For a while, I was the only one living here, and then we were vacationing in Spain last winter. We'll be setting traditions this time around."

Alessandro put his free arm around her shoulders, linking his little family together. He wanted everything to be perfect for the holidays. "What traditions do you wish to set?"

"Maybe we *should* go to Joe's Christmas Eve party," she said softly. "It's important to be part of the community. Robin needs to grow up knowing there are so many people worth loving, whether they call it Yule or Christmas or Saturnalia like those old Roman vampires."

Alessandro nodded his agreement, then kissed her, tasting toothpaste. Vampires didn't officially do Christmas—or whatever equivalent they'd observed during their human lives—but most never lost the instinct for a winter party. Joe's decision to host his chosen family and friends was perfectly natural, especially since so many of their community didn't have blood relatives nearby.

Robin, warm and sweet-smelling, sagged against him with a yawn. Holly leaned into him from the other side, soft and feminine. Alessandro could have remained there for hours, a pillar to his girls. For as a vampire—or even as a man—he was so exceptionally, gloriously blessed.

He gazed down into his baby girl's face. A strange lurching sensation seemed to suspend time for a moment as he stared into her sleepy green eyes. She was going to be beautiful. Of course, every father thought that about his child, but she had Holly's genes.

There was something from the Caravelli side, too. His family was all tall and fair-haired, and his curly-headed sisters had turned the heads of every village boy. Once Robin grew up, he was going to be a busy man fending off her suitors. It made him smile and grind his teeth at the same time.

"Well, I guess we should send Joe an RSVP," Holly said. "Or maybe I should just phone. We don't have much time, and I have a demon to exorcize."

That reminded Alessandro of what Hazel had said about the demon growing stronger the closer they got to the holidays. "How many days until Christmas Eve?"

"Today's Thursday—well, technically it's Friday morning. The party's Monday."

By the expression on Holly's face, she understood why he'd asked. The demon would be even stronger when she confronted it later that day. Not a good thought to take to bed. He pulled the subject back to the holidays, hoping to ease her worry.

"I had better start my shopping."

Holly took a step back, raising one eyebrow. "You haven't even begun?"

He shrugged. "I don't like to rush."

"All the same, you'd better get going." She stood on her toes to kiss his cheek. "But not tonight. We have to put the princess to bed. In fact, I'm more than ready to be tucked in myself."

Suddenly, things were looking up. "My pleasure."

CHAPTER 5

This is Errata Jones signing off the late show at CSUP, coming to you from the University of Fairview campus in the wee hours. Safe travels, my friends, and remember there are only a few shopping days left to go. Don't let your tree go untrimmed. Get out there and make merry.

Admit it—human, werebeast, Undead, or just unhinged, we all love a party. But as with everything, there's a dark side to this season. It's the long winter night of reckoning. Have you been good this year? Bad? Somewhere in between? Will good old Saint Nick bring you sugarplums or will his evil twin Krampus hunt you down for a spanking? We won't know until the sleigh arrives. All we can do is lose ourselves in the revelry and hope for the best. Carpe noctem, and all that.

But as for now, this little werekitty is ready to lay down her sleepy head. Night, night, my loves.

FRIDAY AFTERNOON, Holly declared war on the purple goop demon. Since Ashe's husband was out of town on a business trip, they left Grandma and the kids with Perry's extended family.

There was no place safer and more child friendly than with a pack of protective werewolves.

Once that was done, reconnaissance began. First, they took a long drive around the neighborhood, searching for anything odder than usual in a corner of the downtown largely populated with supernatural creatures. The car radio was tuned to CSUP, the daytime announcer chattering on about non-toxic chew toys for shifter children.

"Perry's in love with the host, you know?" Ashe said, nodding toward the radio.

"Oscar?" Holly asked, wrinkling her nose. "I thought he was married."

Ashe gave her a big-sister look of disgust. She was tall and fair-haired, as athletic as Holly was bookish. "Errata Jones."

Holly shrugged. Every warm-blooded male—and a few Undead ones—were in love with the werecougar night host of CSUP. "They're friends."

"Yeah, and they'll stay that way unless he makes a move." Ashe turned another corner, narrowly avoiding a bike courier. "I don't think she'd mind."

Holly sipped her takeout latté. "How do you know all of this?"

Ashe gave her a sideways look. "I have informants."

"Your running club?"

"Maybe." Ashe worked out with a handful of women, not all of them human. Keeping up with shifters and vampires was punishing, but then Ashe was hardcore that way.

"When did you turn into such a gossip?"

"I'm the mother of a teenager. Maybe it's rubbing off on me."

Ashe parked her SUV across the street from the community center. The two sisters sat in the car for a moment, studying the building. The windows were boarded up with plywood, but otherwise it appeared perfectly ordinary.

"I'm not fooled," Holly said. "The neighborhood looks quiet enough, but this place isn't clean."

"Nope," her sister replied. "Grandma might have burned her cards, but the demon got in here once. It can get in again."

With that, Ashe got out of the car. Rather than coffee, she was swigging something bright green that smelled like grass clippings. She finished the drink, made a face, and tossed the travel mug into the backseat before slamming the door.

"Why don't you just get an Americano and have it over with?" Holly asked.

"I'm on a detox. No junk food, no sugar, no caffeine."

"I know a mild enchantment you could use."

"I'm doing this the old-fashioned way. It takes dedication to be this bad-assed," Ashe said, indicating her lean form. "The life of a slayer increases wear and tear. I need to be proactive."

"Does that make slayer years like dog years? You're like two hundred and ten and ready to be put down?"

Ashe snorted. "You wish. This bad girl has plenty of mileage yet."

She started across the street with a long-legged swagger. Holly grabbed her knapsack and followed, feeling once again like the good little girl tagging after her intriguingly naughty older sibling.

The sign on the main door said the center was closed due to a plumbing emergency, but Alessandro had borrowed the key the night before. Holly unlocked the door, then punched in the alarm code she had written on a sticky note.

Once inside, they found the bingo room immediately because of the yellow police tape strung across the doorway—as sheriff of the local supernatural community, Alessandro kept a roll in the trunk of his car. Ashe tore it down and they slowly went through, watchful for any movement. As advertised, the place smelled of rot. Ashe turned a little pale at the stink.

Holly's shoes crunched on the debris littering the floor tiles. With a sinking heart, she catalogued the damage to the room. Besides the broken window and furnishings, the ceiling and walls were discolored. "Look," she said, pointing. "That must be where the slime ate through the paint."

"Al was right." Ashe pulled a fork from the woodwork. "Our monster likes to throw things."

"Don't call him Al. Not where he can hear you, anyway."

Her sister grinned. "If he wants to be one of the family, he's got to loosen up a little."

"Proceed at your own risk."

"He just doesn't realize he likes me yet."

Holly rolled her eyes, then got back to work.

The condition of the floor was unspeakable. The only items that had survived were the scruffy artificial tree in the corner and the stockings thumbtacked to the far wall.

Ashe picked up a fallen bingo card. "Bad luck for someone. They were a letter off from winning."

"I know Grandma's tough," Holly said, "but this must have been a horrific scene." The evidence was that her grandmother hadn't insisted on coming with them that day. She'd been uncharacteristically quiet when the sisters had dropped her off with Perry's family.

Ashe's expression was arctic. "We'll make sure the demon doesn't bother her again."

A finger of anxiety ran down Holly's spine. She'd battled demons before—one had been a master of terrifying strength—and so far, she'd been lucky. By all accounts, this one was nowhere as powerful. That didn't mean defeating it would be a walk in the park.

She drew an elastic from her pocket, hastily pulling her hair into a ponytail. The gesture was a habit, something she did before a job. Then she began whispering a chant to cast a detection spell. As she held her right palm out flat, a cloud formed above it like a miniature thunderhead. When it had grown to the size of a baseball, Holly was satisfied. A gentle puff of her breath sent it floating toward the ceiling.

"I've never seen that spell before," Ashe said, clearly impressed.

"It's one I picked up from an old journal Auntie Rose left in the library when she moved away. If there's demonic energy present, the cloud will turn dark."

Her sister frowned. "What does that tell us? We already know a demon was here."

"Timing is everything. If it goes dark right away, we know the banishment failed."

Ashe fell silent. The cloud drifted aimlessly, bumping from one corner of the ceiling to another. They stood shoulder to shoulder, watching it go. Before long, sparkles accumulated on the spell's surface, giving it the appearance of a disco ball.

"Freaky," Ashe said. "How bad is it?"

"I'm not sure. I've never seen a demon that sparkled," Holly said uneasily. She'd encountered a soul-eater and a collector demon, but they'd behaved like proper hellspawn. An evil entity that looked like tinsel and sang Christmas carols was—confusing.

"Can we nuke it?" Ashe asked, ever the slayer.

She didn't wait for an answer, but circled the room, clearing it of potential weapons. Since the demon liked to hurl objects at high velocity, that meant everything had to be removed. Holly joined her, stacking the chairs and tables in the hallway. Soon, the room was almost entirely bare, only the decorations left behind. Ash found a broom, then began sweeping away the debris on the floor. Small shards of broken china could be dangerous at high speeds.

A glass ornament rolled away, bouncing gently off the baseboards. Holly twitched, impatient to get on with the ritual.

"Nervous?" Ashe asked.

"A bit." Facing the demon was only part of it. "This may sound crazy, but I just remembered I have to pick up milk on the way home. If I'm thinking about that right now, I have too much on my mind."

She was always busy, but this time of year was nuts. A voice nagged in the back of her mind, reminding her that she had shopping to do. There was dry-cleaning to pick up, client phone calls to return, wrapping, and…

There was always too much to do. Witch or not, she was a student and a working mother with the same problems as any other woman with a toddler. Alessandro more than pulled his weight, but whatever she was doing, two more things were nagging for attention. It was hard not to feel inadequate.

Ashe was leaning on the broom, staring at her with green eyes almost exactly like her own. "You can be supermom some other day," she said, reading her far too well. "Today, you focus on the demon."

Ashe's words needled, but she was right. There was a demon. This wasn't the time to rush or cut corners, however many boxes Holly had to check that day. Fresh guilt nagged at her.

"You work yourself to the bone," Ashe pointed out.

"I've been very lucky in my life. I try to deserve it."

"Lighten up on yourself a little. You're only lucky if you actually enjoy the gifts the Goddess sends you."

Holly laughed, but silently admitted Ashe was right. Instead of arguing, she unpacked her knapsack, bringing out the tools of her trade. Grandma had left the spell circle, so all they had to do was reactivate it when they began the exorcism. For the next steps, Holly brought out her strongest spell mixtures. Since there were no elderly bystanders in the room, there was no need to hold back.

As she unwrapped her equipment, a prickling sensation between her shoulder blades made her hunch like a turtle retreating into its shell. A sinking feeling of anxiety grew in the pit of her stomach.

"What's going on with the decorations?" Ashe asked, finishing her sweeping job and returning to Holly's side.

Holly looked up. They were scattered on the floor instead of hanging on the tree. Uneasily, she tried to remember if that was where they'd been before.

"Maybe the center staff was packing them away?" Holly ventured, fairly certain she was wrong. "I doubt they'll be using this room again before Christmas."

Ashe glared at the balls and bells and fake gingerbread men. Then Holly noticed her counting and asked why.

"The decorations moved." Her sister pointed an accusing finger. "A minute ago, they were a dozen floor tiles away. Now there are eleven squares between them and us."

"Seriously? That's so B-movie." A miasma of dread crawled over her.

"No kidding."

Wordlessly, Holly snatched the broom from Ashe and began walking clockwise, waking the protective circle as she went. She tried to ignore the delicate rumble of the glass ornaments as they rolled across the tile toward her. It should have been an innocent sound, but it sent spider's legs up her spine. Closing the circle, she set down the broom.

"Holly," Ashe whispered.

The sisters stood within the ring of protection. Ashe grasped Holly's hand as if they were little girls again. The decorations had reached the outside of the circle, the felt gingerbread men standing on flimsy feet, the reindeer prancing in place. Fear danced at the edge of Holly's mind as she heard the distant ring of childish laughter. Ashe swore under her breath.

"It can't get inside your head unless you make a place for it," Holly said. But even as she uttered the words, her anxiety spiked. *You're just a fraud, a fake, and there's no way you can defeat even a tiny demon, much less this one.*

Her mouth went dry, her pulse quickening until she grew dizzy. *Stop,* she thought. *Stop.* Those feelings were real, but they were ordinary insecurities—the crazy talk anyone had in their head on a bad day. The demon had made those naggy little voices so much bigger.

You're a bad mother. You should be with your child, not showing off your powers here. Stop being so selfish. The voices seemed to be coming from the tiny stitched mouths of the gingerbread men, even though Holly knew they were inside her head.

"Make them stop staring," Ashe said between clenched teeth. "It's like being interrogated."

"Push them out of your head," Holly said. "See what they really are. Just pieces of cloth and plastic." Taking her own advice, she carefully quieted her emotions. No point in giving the hellspawn the fuel it wanted.

And then she turned her attention back to the circle of toys. The demonic energy animating the decorations gave them an expectant quality that reminded her of a child—one who had become entranced by a shiny object. There was something charming in it, but also raw, unfiltered hunger. Children didn't understand cost or practicality, just that they *wanted*. She'd seen it in Robin, who could barely walk or talk but was still glued to the TV commercials with that purple unicorn toy. Every child demanded Frederick the Unicorn for Christmas this year. Children had few memories to take, but Holly bet their desire would be pure and sweet to the demon.

Holly shook herself. She was losing focus again. *See? You aren't half the witch you think you are.* The decorations teetered on the edge of the circle, almost strong enough to cross over. The ravenous energy was practically thick enough to touch. All at once, Holly ran out of patience.

"Oh, no you don't," she said, picking up the broom again.

"What are you doing?" Ashe demanded.

By way of reply, Holly gripped her sister's hand so tightly she felt the bones shift. She hadn't had time to light candles or burn incense, but she couldn't take another moment of the demon whispering in her head. She was holding her ground for now, but sooner or later, her confidence would suffer. With her free hand, she thrust the broom into the air like a lightning rod. Sometimes a witch cast a circle with all the ceremony of a royal tea party. Other times, she sent up a flare. "East! South! West! North! Attend!"

Light blazed around the raised tip of the broom handle, radiating in a corona of reds and blues and greens. As it grew stronger, it fell in veils to the edges of the circle, forming a coruscating cone of protective power. Holly felt it vibrate in her bones, like a long, low note so deep it escaped hearing. She drew in a breath, finally free of suffocating doubt. *I can do this.*

And so could Ashe. Her slayer's strength hummed like an enormous generator, steady and strong. Holly drew on that energy, weaving it with her own to double her power. Slowly, deliberately, she lowered the broom to the ground at her feet. "I summon and entreat you, Spirit, to heal us, to heal this place, and to cast out this intruder. Send this malevolence back where it belongs."

The words were simple and to the point, her intent perfectly clear. The instant the straws of the broom touched the tile, pure white light blazed from under their feet. It shot in searing rays to touch every corner of the room, as if they stood on a star.

It was too bright. Holly squeezed her eyes shut, but the afterimage remained. Tears streamed down her face, some from pure relief. Holly felt Ashe's strong arms around her, and she had a fleeting image from her childhood, from before their parents had died. Ashe and Holly had been two girls making angels in the snow, their faces flushed with cold and laughter. Icicles had hung from the eaves of the Carver house, and the sky had been a pure, cloudless blue. It had been just days before the Yule, and presents were under the tree. A bright, sacred spirit had seemed to jewel everything like sunlit frost.

That Yule had been Holly's yardstick, a limitless gift she went back to when she needed a dose of happiness. That healing power was the good, strong side of the season that shone all year no matter what. Holly hung onto the vision for as long as she could, savoring it until the ragged parts of her heart no longer ached. It reminded her of all those she loved, that she was loved, and that the world was fundamentally good.

When she finally released the circle, the air held the pure, sweet scent of a winter forest.

"I WON," Holly said later that afternoon, lifting her latté in a salute.

Perry raised an eyebrow. "Did you doubt your victory?"

Holly stalled, sipping the foamy coffee.

Perry pointed a finger. "You have just as much performance anxiety as the rest of us."

She shrugged. "I'm just a girl with a broom."

"Who kicks demon tail."

"I try my best. That wasn't the strongest hellspawn I've ever faced, but it was sneaky."

Holly checked her watch, but she still had a few minutes to relax. Ashe had gone to retrieve Grandma and the kids. Holly was at the Empire Hotel delivering her report to Perry. The pub-style restaurant was packed and noisy, with every table filled—and no wonder. As well as being a good place to eat, the old hotel had plenty of atmosphere, with stained glass, a rolled-tin ceiling, and antique fixtures. Behind the old-fashioned bar with its brass rail, mirrored shelving reflected an impressive array of bottles. All it needed was costumed actors to bring back the gold-rush days. Then again, some of the clientele remembered that era perfectly well.

Holly set down her cup. "I admit it was strange how it found my insecurities so fast. I've been worried about keeping every-thing together—the Three Sisters Agency, schoolwork, and home —with the added workload of the holidays."

"And that's what it used against you?"

"The emotions around it, for sure. Yet, it seemed to be banished by remembering my best Yule of all."

Perry frowned, intensity filling his lean face. "While that seems right, it also seems wrong."

"Why?"

"I'm not sure, but wouldn't it be better *not* to have a holiday-themed solution, given what we're dealing with?"

"I dunno." She understood what he meant, even if she didn't fully agree. There was no chance to explore the point because Joe Trenchen, the hotel's owner and chief bartender, sat at their table.

"Hello," he said, flashing a smile.

Joe was tall, dark, and cursed. Holly had never learned all the details about that curse, but guessed he was almost as old as Alessandro. He was also, arguably, the most handsome man in Fairview, with near-black eyes and lean features that might have put him on a magazine cover. Any number of women, and not a few men, had tried to catch his attention. But while he was an excellent listener behind the bar, he remained intensely private about his personal affairs.

"Hi, Joe," Holly said. "It looks like you're having a busy holiday season."

He gave a casual shrug. "We're doing all right. Did you get my invite for the twenty-fourth? I'm going to close to the public and just have family and friends."

Holly made her decision. "We received it, and we'll be there as long as it's okay to bring Robin."

Joe's smile widened. "Absolutely bring the little charmer. This is a child friendly event. I'm setting up a special supervised play-room for the kids."

He looked truly happy as he said it, in a way Holly hadn't seen before. Perhaps this party, centered on his closest friends, was a gift that filled his needs as much as those of his guests. The thought made her glad she'd accepted.

"What about you?" Joe asked Perry. "I realize there might be a conflict with a pack function."

"Well…" Perry suddenly looked shifty, which was odd for him. "I'm not sure yet about my plus one."

Joe's eyes were bright as he leaned forward, mischief plain on his face. "I take it you have some options in mind?" For someone who was closed-mouthed about his personal business, Joe certainly enjoyed meddling in everyone else's.

Perry gave him a quelling glare.

"Could it be the lovely Errata Jones?" Joe asked.

That piqued Holly's interest. What had Ashe said earlier?

Perry made a disgusted noise. "She's a friend, a good friend, but no."

All the same, his ears turned pink.

"Why not?" Joe asked, running a thumbnail along a crack in the old table. "Just because she's a werecougar and you're a werewolf, that doesn't mean you can't attend the same Christmas party. Have some fun."

Perry's brow furrowed. "Even if this were a welcome topic of discussion—which it's not—have you ever tried to get a decision from a cat shifter?"

"Cats always say no until they say yes. You just need to be patient."

Something in Perry's expression said he'd had enough. Holly stepped in. "Who else is bringing children?"

Joe listed some families. A few had kids close to Robin's age. "The one thing I won't have in here is that purple unicorn," he said with disgust.

"The one on TV?" Perry rolled his eyes. "My nieces and nephews are hypnotized by that thing. They advertise it every five minutes during the cartoons."

Joe made a face. "I heard there were fist fights in the big box stores on Black Friday. Parents are desperate to put them under the tree.

"The kids will probably lose interest by New Year's," Perry said.

"Robin is young yet, thank heavens," Holly said. "It'll be a few years before she completely understands about Santa Claws and Yuletide stockings."

Perry checked his watch, one of the fancy ones with multiple dials. "I promised my sister I'd pick up my nephews from hockey practice. Would you like me to drop you home?"

"Thanks." Holly finished her coffee. "I look forward to the party, Joe."

Chairs scraped on the wooden floor and shopping bags rustled. Soon, Holly was outside, the cold sea air chasing away the scents of the pub. Perry seemed pensive. Holly guessed he was still thinking about Errata Jones.

"The heart is an inexplicable thing," she offered. "Alessandro and I don't make much sense to people, but I wouldn't change what we have for the world."

"Ignore what Joe said." Perry's smile was tight. "The cat and I are just friends. That's strange enough by anyone's standards. Besides, I've been dating someone else."

"Are you going to bring this other person instead?"

"No." He shook his head. "That wouldn't work out."

Holly took a breath to argue, but in the end, she held her peace. Perry was very, very smart, and sometimes that was the worst kind of dumb.

CHAPTER 6

"Don't you want to go see Santa Claws?" Errata asked the next afternoon in her husky, teasing voice.

"Meh," Perry Baker replied, still grumpy at the prospect of crowds and gift-giving decisions. Plus, it was cold, gray, and rainy—a typical December day in the Pacific Northwest.

"Where's your boundless holiday spirit?" She turned into the parking lot outside the Fairview Sports and Recreation Center. It was the final day of the Yuletide Holiday Market, an arts and crafts event by and for the local supernatural community. "Counting today, there's only three shopping days till Christmas."

"I really hope you're not going to make me sit on Santa's knee."

"I don't think so, darling. That would be weird, even for us."

Errata swung her Jaguar coupe into the last parking space, beating out a massive pickup by a whisker. The truck made a sound like a startled dinosaur as it lurched to a stop on the frosty pavement. Turning off the Jaguar's ignition, Errata smoothed her chin-length, jet-black hair, then glanced in the rearview mirror, looking pleased with herself. Perry twisted in his seat to see the pickup driver turn a Christmassy scarlet and lurch off.

Perry willed his heart to resume its normal rhythm. Errata was a werecougar, and there were reasons cats shouldn't drive. Werewolves like him were another matter. Wolves appreciated order, including stop signs. Cats did things because they could—like pester him into going to this stupid craft fair.

That was what he got for befriending a feline. He cast her a sidelong look, taking in her high cheekbones and smooth, golden skin. It was all he could do not to reach over and stroke her hair, but that would be crossing a boundary. She'd made it clear from the start that cats walked alone.

Errata finished preening and gave him an arch look. "Shouldn't you be shopping for your human, what's-her-name?"

Perry released his seatbelt. "Her name is Tiffani. With an *i*."

"Tiffani. Of course it is." Errata patted his cheek with pity. "Come on. First fifty guests get a goodie bag."

"She's fun," Perry said, sounding defensive even to himself.

"Humans generally are," she said agreeably. "You should buy her something really nice."

"Men don't shop before December twenty-fourth," he protested as he got out of the car.

"Friends don't let friends give their sweethearts, even ones named Tiffani with an *i*, gift cards."

"But gift cards make sense."

Errata flung the end of her scarf over her shoulder with a flick of one gloved hand. "Be grateful you have me to watch over you." After she clicked the locks, she swept toward the entrance of the building, leaving Perry to catch up.

"Cats," he grumbled. "What do you want for Yule?"

"Not a gift card."

Plenty of people turned to stare as she passed. She was the late-night talk show host of CSUP 101.5 FM radio—*The station that put the super in supernatural!*—and that made her a celebrity in their insular world. Her black-and-white coat flared as she moved, framing her high-heeled boots and tight red sweater. She looked like the naughty list made flesh, but in an elegant and untouchable way.

Perry trotted after her, certain he was exactly where she wanted him. They pushed through the glass doors of the recreation center, which smelled of wet coats and freshly brewed coffee. His mood improved when he saw a friend at the admission table. "I see the hellhounds are doing their bit for the community, and probably eating all the shortbread."

"I would expect nothing less, on both counts," said Lore, the leader of the local hellhound pack. He was large, looming, and slightly feral, but today he wore a set of fuzzy reindeer antlers with bells. He took their money, then handed them tickets for the door prize draw. "How's end of term? I didn't think you'd see the light of day for another week at least."

Perry shrugged. "Last class was Monday. Now I just have to mark a kajillion papers." He taught computer science at the university, which had both human and non-human faculty and students. "At least this year, the exam schedule avoided the full moon."

"You mean the kids can't claim to have gone furry and eaten their homework?"

"They'll find an excuse for a bad grade." Perry shrugged. "It's part of the student experience."

Lore shook his head as if to say the world was a sad and sorry place, but the jingling antlers ruined the effect.

"When does Santa Claws arrive?" Errata asked, smiling as a trio of tiny light fae children scampered by.

"He arrived about an hour ago. He'll be here until dusk. After that, we'll shut down the children's area and set up for the vampires." Lore folded his arms. "Apparently, the hot stocking stuffer this year is fake human teeth."

With that, Perry and Errata took their goody bags and raffle tickets, moving into the cheerful chaos of the market. The three fae girls in their sparkling dresses pushed past again, giggling madly. The fae courts kept to themselves, and to see them mixing with the crowd was rare—and pleasant. The accords between the species were working, bringing peace and prosperity. Even a few years ago, a market like this wouldn't have been possible.

Perry followed as Errata strolled from booth to booth. She seemed unhurried but covered ground at an impressive pace, as if she knew what she wanted and had no time for things that weren't on her list. Perry was nowhere near as focused.

"I think I know how a pinball feels," he grumbled as he collided with yet another distracted customer.

"Use your elbows. Shopping is a contact sport."

"I thought cats stalked, not bulldozed."

"You've never seen a pride of lions at a fresh kill?"

"There's an image I didn't need in my head." Would it be weird to say he found it just a little compelling?

Wedging their way through a tightly packed crowd, they stopped at a booth that sold candy. Perry caught the scent of her skin beneath the sugary cloud of vanilla and pumpkin spice. He rarely got to stand so close and he relished the moment, aware of the energy that always seemed to spark between them—not just in a metaphorical way, either. Her presence was like an electrical charge, tingling against his flesh.

He had an Alpha's iron restraint, and that gave him the ability to hold a job, teach a room full of students, and generally pass for human in a human world. His mild-mannered professor identity was a masterpiece of willpower. Sadly, self-control didn't always extend to his dealings with the cat.

His hand brushed hers, almost by accident. She startled, then withdrew a half-step—only half, because the booth was too crammed for more. "Sorry," he said, his tone saying he wasn't sorry at all.

With only a shadow of a smile, Errata took her change and purchases before dashing back into the throng of shoppers. That was the way she kept her distance, always one step out of reach.

She never challenged him, but she never gave in, either. Friends. A line he couldn't cross. Nothing more.

Yet, he'd just put a paw over the line. Maybe Holly—and Joe and Grandma Carver and a dozen others—were right. He couldn't ignore the attraction between them forever. Perry turned and followed Errata, aware his hunter's instinct was roused. Maybe it was Yuletide, or exams, or the fact he needed a lot more coffee, but his wolf was winning today. It wanted to chase.

Lucky for the cat, she'd stopped moving. With awestruck wonder, she pointed to a table overflowing with toys. "Do you see that?"

"Yeah." He grinned.

She grabbed Perry's sleeve and dragged him over, all her dignified poise falling away. The table was heaped with glittering puffs of fuzz the size of soccer balls. Snatching one up, she tossed it at him. It floated weightlessly for an instant, drifting in the air currents like a possessed tutu. Perry stood for a moment, hands shoved in his pockets, trying to be the bored male dragged on a shopping expedition—but he couldn't help himself. He batted it back. She sent it spinning into the air again, her eyes wide as they followed the mesmerizing toy.

"Hey!" the witch running the stall said. "Are you buying that?"

Perry caught it, trying—but failing—to assume an air of professorial dignity. Errata stood close, her shoulder brushing his as color mantled her cheeks. They probably looked like a pair of guilty children, but all he saw was her beauty. She was gorgeous, the heat of her body warm against his side. For an instant, she'd forgotten to pull away.

"I think my nieces and nephews would like those toys," Errata said, laughter just under her words.

He handed her the puff with a flourish. "You might have to test them before they go in the mail. I might have to help."

They exchanged a conspiratorial look. Despite their differences, they'd always shared the ability to be silly.

"Better get an extra just in case," Errata murmured. She was suddenly the picture of poise once more, her kittenish mood hidden behind the sleek hair and elegant coat. "My sister's kits are absolute monsters."

"How long are you visiting your family?" Perry asked.

"I'll be gone for three weeks," she replied, stuffing her reusable shopping bag with fluffy balls.

Three weeks seemed like a long time. "I'll miss you."

"You have your pack."

"You're different."

Her shoulders tensed, as if bracing against his words. She raised her green-flecked hazel eyes. "So I should be. I'm not a wolf."

She took off down the row of tables, leaving him there to stew.

Perry strode after. "Errata, wait."

"So, what are you going to buy your lady love?" she asked sweetly. "Your Tiffani with an *i*."

"I don't know," Perry shot back. "And I'm just dating her. She's no more serious than I am."

Errata sighed. "What does she like?"

"She skates in the roller derby."

Errata blinked. "Roller derby?"

Perry had finally surprised her. His smile showed teeth. "Tough girls in short skirts, moving fast. Suitable for chasing. And human. For a werewolf, that rings a lot of bells."

Her eyes narrowed slightly. "You're joking, right?"

"Sadly, no. I'm a dog."

Errata smoothed her hair. "Are you going to invite her home to meet the Alpha?"

"Nope."

"Why not?"

He shrugged. "It's not like that. She's not taking me home to her folks, either."

Errata spun to face him. Ignoring the crowd pushing by, she grabbed his chin and forced him to meet her eyes. As she leaned close, he could feel her warm breath on his skin. "Does she even know what you are?"

Her touch, steel-strong and yet soft, did something to his insides that definitely didn't belong in the friend zone. "I've never discussed my wolf with her."

"No?" Errata's voice swooped up, incredulous.

Perry embraced a hard knot of defiance. "Sometimes it's nice to be ordinary. It's an art form."

Errata was silent for a heartbeat, her nostrils flaring as if she scented something foul. "You're an idiot."

His temper spiked. "Really?"

Her eyes flashed in answer. "You're a professor. The son of the Alpha. One day, you may be the Alpha."

"So?"

"You're financially secure, intelligent, and good-looking. You've nothing to hide. Why waste your time and hers?"

"You think I'm being—what? Unfair? Lazy? Am I setting my sights too low?" His voice edged into a growl.

"I don't need to answer those questions. That's your job." Errata held his gaze for a long moment, finally releasing his chin.

He rubbed it, too angry to speak. Stunned. Maybe even disappointed with himself. He couldn't quite put a name to what he felt, but it struck deep. He felt his beast stir, ears flat and teeth bared. It must have showed, because Errata fell back a few steps.

"Maybe you should tell me why you care," he snapped, making it an accusation instead of a question.

"I need air." She turned and stalked away, coat swishing behind her as she disappeared into the crowd. Again.

His first instinct was to chase her once more, but this time he forced his feet to remain still. What had just happened? Errata was too independent to let him close. And yet, when he befriended a happy, healthy human girl who only wanted a no-strings good time, she objected. It made no sense.

He could have dominated a female wolf. That wasn't always easy, but his veins ran with the blood of Alphas. He knew the rules—what to demand and when to retreat. But a feline? Everything had to be negotiated with a cat. And then re-negotiated, because they changed their minds with the wind.

The crowd ebbed around him in a fast-flowing river, the people blurring together with the lights and tinsel. Perry turned and trudged aimlessly down the row of booths, not caring where he went.

Perhaps he should have pushed harder. Perhaps he should have backed away long ago—but he knew neither was possible. He and Errata were caught in a dance made from their own contrary natures. The magnetic pull of it kept him mesmerized. Even the tension between friendship and unrequited lust kept him as transfixed as a harvest moon.

She was everything. He'd already sailed—at least in spirit—far past any line in the sand she'd drawn. What was he supposed to do about it?

Perry drifted along with the crowd. Although his thoughts turned inward, uneasiness stiffened his shoulders. At first, he put it down to his mood, but then an odd scent caught his attention. Burnt toast?

Perry wheeled, instincts on alert. That was the stink of portal magic. His fists clenched, apprehension rippling down his back. His wolf stirred, alert and troubled.

Nobody opened a hole through time and space without a good reason. In fact, it was usually for a very bad reason. Most the time, something nasty lurked on the other side, like dragons or a mad sorcerer or demonic rabbits. Portal magic had no place in a crowded auditorium, especially one teeming with kids.

A second thought crowded in. Holly had banished the demon

from the community center, but this was prime territory for a creature that thrived on holiday-themed emotion. Perry shoved his way through the crowd, following the scent to its source. It seemed to be coming from the far corner, near the throne where Santa Claws reigned. Red-and-white ropes separated this area from the shopping. To the left was Santa's throne, and to the right was a supervised children's play zone scattered with gym mats and toys. Babysitters in green elf costumes kept watch so parents could leave their brood and enjoy a few minutes in peace.

Perry drew nearer, seeing no signs of trouble. Most of the teenaged elves played on their smartphones while Santa appeared to have gone for coffee.

"They aren't real elves," a childish voice said bitterly. "Those are just dumb hellhounds in outfits."

Perry scanned the area for the speaker. It was a fae boy about eight years old, slumped glumly beside the trio of little girls Perry and Errata had seen running around. The three girls sat cross-legged and held hands, oblivious to the boy's snide remarks. Their dainty pastel dresses shimmered under the fluorescent lights as they chanted, their eyes squeezed shut in concentration. Fae children were small, but he guessed none of the girls could be older than five or six. With sudden, blunt horror he realized they were the ones poking a hole in the universe, and he caught a whiff of peppermint and rot.

Instantly, Perry was over the rope barrier. "Hey, hang on a minute!"

He dropped to one knee beside them. It felt ridiculous, politely asking them to stop. This was a matter for tooth and claw and possibly rocket launchers, but these were babies. Highly magical, dangerous babies. However, if there was one thing the pack understood, it was pups.

The girl in the pale yellow dress opened enormous blue eyes. "Sh, we're contrating," she said gravely.

"Concentrating, stupid," said the boy who had to be her brother. "This is all stupid."

The hellhounds were watching Perry, their eyes glinting red. He was a lone male among children. Normally that would have been enough for hard questions, but they knew Perry and trusted him as Lore's friend. As long as he didn't make a sudden move, everyone was safe.

"What are you concentrating on?" Perry asked the girl, keeping his voice gentle.

"The Santa Claws they have here isn't real," she said in a whisper. "We're asking for the real one. We've been asking for him for *weeks*."

The brother rolled his eyes.

"Are you sure this Santa's not real?" Perry asked seriously, pitching his voice a little louder to distract the girls. He could feel the spell stumbling, but children had amazing focus when they wanted something with all their hearts.

"Of course he's not," said one of the others.

"How do you know?" Perry asked. The crawling sensation down his back grew faint. The spell had finally collapsed under the weight of his interruption. The smell of peppermint faded away.

His thoughts pinwheeled, and he fought a sudden urge to laugh hysterically. Wasn't asking for Santa the same as summoning him? Was this how the demon had first appeared just weeks ago? The timeline fit—and baby fae hyped on the holidays would supply all the psychic charge this demon required. *Fenrir's furry balls!*

"This Santa doesn't even have wings," said the first girl with disapproval.

Given that Santa was played by Perry's old Uncle Bob, this was true.

"That's the Winter Fairy who has wings," the brother said acidly. "Santa Claws is just a wolf who hangs out with a bunch of elves. He probably eats them. Two bites and they're gone, nom nom."

With that, the smallest fairy girl started to cry, fat tears rolling down her cheeks and dripping onto her sparkling pink dress. That was too much for Perry. He gathered up the tiny girl and rose, holding her against his chest and stroking her back the way he would one of the pack's pups. The difference was she was nowhere near as sturdy. It was like comforting a baby bird.

"Hush," he whispered, rocking her. She smelled like chocolate and the faint, sweet musk of the very young.

"I don't want to be eaten by Santa Claws," she mumbled into his shirt. She was crying with abandon now, clearly in need of a nap. "He eats bad girls and boys."

"Nah," Perry said. "If that were true, I'd have been lunch ten times over."

She seemed to find that amusing. Tears turned to silvery giggles that finished in a hiccup. It was only then Perry noticed the very tall male fae standing mere feet away. Her father, by the scowl clouding his patrician features. Wordlessly, the fae held out his arms.

Perry promptly handed the child over, and she curled against her father's shoulder like a kitten. Daddy Fae regarded Perry with obvious suspicion while the older children crowded around him, most barely reaching his waist.

It was a tricky moment. Light fae were notoriously touchy, especially when it came to strangers from outside their clans. "Your girls were summoning Santa Claws," Perry offered. "I intervened."

An exasperated expression crossed the male's face that made him look very much like his son. "Again? I'll be glad when the holidays are over."

Perry's jaw dropped a little. "You're aware they've done this before?"

"They try. Fortunately, they don't know the exact incantations." His voice was deep and melodious, but edged with frustration. "It's been going on ever since the first holiday special on television, sponsoring that wretched sparkling purple unicorn. The advertisers never consider the wear and tear on parents."

"I guess not." Perry forced a smile. "Say, did you know there was a holiday-themed demon showing up in the neighborhood?"

The father's eyebrows slanted in unhappy surprise. "Really?"

Perry chose his words carefully. "A friend of mine sent it back to its own dimension, but just in case…"

"Are you saying my daughters summoned a demon?" Color rose along the fae's sharp cheekbones.

"Maybe not," Perry said quickly, avoiding a direct accusation. "But they might attract its attention."

That seemed to soothe the fae's temper. "Good to know. I deplore it when such creatures get in the house."

"Yeah," Perry said. "It's hard to get the smell out."

It was hard to know if the fae detected sarcasm, because his expression never changed. "I thank you for your assistance. I'll ensure nothing like this happens again."

Then the man turned to speak to his wife, who had just arrived. The little girl opened her wide blue eyes, then peeped over her father's shoulder at Perry.

"May Santa Claws grant your wish," she whispered so softly it took a wolf's hearing to catch the words.

Perry smiled and waved as they left, momentarily lost in those blue eyes. And then he turned, seeing Errata watching him from the other side of the rope barrier. His heart stopped at the soft look on her face. She tilted her head to one side a moment, considering him while a smile played over her lips. A strange sensation came over Perry, leaving him at once energized and weak in the knees.

"You wouldn't believe…" he began.

"I brought you hot chocolate," she interrupted softly, raising a paper cup.

Food was her way of apologizing. Perry stepped over the rope barrier, leaving the play area behind, and accepted the drink. It was mounded with whipped cream and marshmallows. "Thanks."

"You're going to make a wonderful Alpha," she said. "You know how to charm as well as fight."

"I'll need more than a high approval rating with preschoolers."

One corner of her mouth curled up. "Maybe not. Kids are painfully honest."

They were standing barely inches apart, the rims of their cups almost touching. Errata heaved a breath that wasn't quite a sigh, then caught his gaze and held it. "Ever since I've known you, you've chased women who couldn't possibly make you happy. There was that vampire, then the one with the stakes. Now Tiffani. Why do you do it?" Her eyes were hypnotic, the full force of her beast behind them.

"Maybe I like challenging women."

"You think *they're* a challenge?" She blinked once, her expression between amused and incredulous. "They're kid's stuff. It's time you had the real thing."

She leaned forward, keeping the steaming cups of chocolate perfectly steady, and kissed him. There was no preamble, no testing, no more dance. Her lips pressed hot against his, rich with creamy chocolate and all the sensuality that was Errata Jones. Her tongue begged for entrance and he welcomed her, bewildered but relishing the silky promise of her mouth. Her free hand pressed against his cheek, warm and possessive.

She'd come to him on her own terms. Claimed what she wanted. Gave nothing she didn't value. If he held her, it was because she wanted it at long last.

"Why?" he asked, turning her question back on her. Her expression said she knew what he meant. Why did she care? Why kiss him now?

"Maybe it's time I saved you from yourself." She peeked up

from under her dark lashes. "Or maybe I'm done playing with my prey."

He waited for more, one eyebrow arched.

She frowned. "I want you. I deserve you. Those others will never appreciate what they've got."

"You're jealous!"

Her chin jerked up. "Don't get carried away."

"You like me. Maybe more than a little."

"Is that a question?" She did her best to look haughty, but couldn't hide a grin.

He laughed, but it wasn't to mock her. He could be humble, because she'd given him an amazing gift. Beneath his own merriment, there was the chime of a little girl's giggle. Maybe it was imagination, but Perry wasn't taking anything for granted.

Errata sipped her chocolate, cream clinging to the bow of her lip. She licked it off, sending his brain into a spiral. "So, what do you want for Yule?"

Perry put his arm around her waist. "I think I've got my present already."

She snuggled closer, touching him nose to nose. With her heels, they were the same height. "Is that it? You're done now? You're not asking for anything else?"

"Never. I want it all. I want it always."

She gave her crooked smile. "Even if it's a challenge?"

He kissed her again, making it last. "I don't do gift cards."

CHAPTER 7

*V*ampires were very capable of worry, especially when they were mated to kick-ass witches. If Alessandro could have built a massive fortress to protect his family…well, Holly wouldn't put up with it, so he may as well not go down that rabbit hole. To be honest, he wouldn't want to rein her in. But the idea of her wrangling that demon turned his cold blood even chillier. She'd handled it, as she'd handled worse, and that made him both terrified and proud. His woman was a peerless magical warrior.

He would do his best to be worthy of her—and tonight that meant leaving her to soak in the bathtub while Grandma spoiled Robin for an hour or two. He'd brought her takeout Thai food—her favorite—a bottle of Chardonnay, and bath oil from the new spa downtown. Sometimes loving a woman meant leaving her to unwind in peace and quiet. He'd remind her of the joys of partnership once he got home.

He strolled Fairview's supernatural district, his thoughts bouncing between Holly's escapades and the fact he had barely started his shopping. Holly had reminded him that his half of the Santa team had better get busy. Inspiration had sparked—at least for Holly's present. He was still working on stocking stuffers for both his girls.

The walk was slow but pleasant. He was off duty, but people still wanted to chat and he was happy to oblige. Everywhere, the mood was as mellow as the street was picturesque. Wreaths hung from old-fashioned lamp standards, pine boughs framed the frosted windows, and music poured from every doorway.

Alessandro pulled his crumpled shopping list out of his pocket, checking his progress, but the holiday scene inevitably took him back to the demon at bingo night. Something about the hellspawn wearing the face of his father still stung like an open wound. The talk shows were correct—daddy issues never quite went away,. Somehow, the demon had sensed that, but there was little it could say that Alessandro hadn't already pondered.

But, vampire or not, he would be different. He would love and protect his girl to the last ounce of his Undead strength and give her the security and stability he'd never had. He would give her the best Christmases ever.

In that spirit, he felt compelled to take one last sweep of the shops. Perhaps a last perfect gift was waiting to be wrapped and put under the tree. Just as he stuffed the list back into his pocket, he saw the Alpha of the hellhounds coming his way. Lore was laden with shopping bags and a harried expression.

"Having a last-minute consumer moment?" Alessandro asked.

"I'm doing better than last year," Lore replied. "At least I didn't wait until Christmas Eve."

"How is Talia?" Lore's mate was another vampire.

"She's helping to put on a children's play," the Alpha replied. "The pups were starting to act out, so we came up with something to keep them busy. The young ones get overexcited this time of year. It's not a good time to be a slipper."

Alessandro eyed the shopping bags. "Did you find everything you were looking for?"

"No. They're all out of the purple unicorns."

"The what?"

"Frederick the Unicorn. This year's *it* toy. They're all over the television. Every kid is about ready to murder to get one, and, consequently, so are their parents."

"A purple unicorn?" A faint bell was sounding in his memory. Holly had said something about Robin getting mesmerized by a character from her cartoons.

Lore shook his head. "They say that supernaturals are all about the forces of evil. I think it's sponsored by breakfast cereal and toy manufacturers."

"I'm out of my depth."

"Every parent thinks that. The preschool years are a game of survival."

Unsettled, Alessandro changed tack. "Are you going to Joe's dinner?"

"Absolutely. Good food, good company."

"Then I will see you there," Alessandro said, cheered by the prospect. "Good luck with your presents."

Lore took his leave and Alessandro turned toward the toy store, certain Robin would like Frederick the Unicorn as a gift. The idea aroused his predatory instinct. He was a hunter and here was something to hunt, a treat to provide for his young.

The toy store window was filled with the familiar array of stuffed animals, action figures, and puzzles. There was so much to choose from and more than any child could possibly enjoy. Alessandro's village had seen nothing like this. Back then, childhood was brief. He'd worked for his bread by the time he was eight. His Robin, however, would have education, choices, and the support to decide who she would become. And love. He had an infinite amount of that for his girl and her extraordinary mother.

A family exiting the store broke his concentration, and he went inside to be engulfed by the warmth. The store was small and crowded, and he spent some time studying the items on the shelves. Eventually, a clerk approached.

"Can I help you?" she asked. She was young with short brown hair and pale blue eyes that marked her as some sort of shifter.

"Do you have Frederick the Unicorn?" he asked.

Her face scrunched as she laughed. "Oh no, we sold out of that days ago. To be quite honest, I'm not sure you could find one anywhere in the city."

That was a challenge if he ever heard one. "Are you sure? There's no chance of ordering it from someplace else?"

"Let me double check," she said with a patience that said she was used to dealing with exasperated parents. She went behind the desk, then began tapping on her computer. "I know the big online retailers have Frederick on backorder, but maybe there's something in one of our sister stores."

Grateful, Alessandro came around the desk to peer over her shoulder. He was invading her space, but he was curious to see what this highly desired toy looked like. When it flashed up on the screen, puzzlement stabbed through him. Frederick was purple and a unicorn, but that was about all that could be said in its defense. The toy had googly eyes and a sparkling pink mane that stuck out at all angles, as if someone had experimented with high-voltage wires.

"What does it do?" he asked doubtfully.

"Do?" the clerk asked. "Nothing, really. I'm sorry, there are none in our system. You might be able to get one in January, but not in time for Christmas."

Alessandro thanked her and left the store. As soon as he hit the street, his competitive instincts flared. Was he going to give up providing for his daughter after visiting just one shop? What kind of a father was he?

It was a half hour before stores started closing, so he moved with vampire speed to the mall several blocks away. There was a toy store at the south end promising thousands of items at discount prices. When there were no Fredericks on display, he compelled the clerk just in case there was a unicorn hidden away on hold, but no.

He approached a third store, running in just as it was closing. "Do you have Frederick the Unicorn?"

The clerk gave a snort of vaguely hysterical laughter. "Good luck. We sold our last one a week ago."

For an instant, Alessandro considered snapping the young man's neck as a punishment for bad service. Truly, stores should train their staff. But he let the retail minion live, mostly because burying bodies was a chore.

Sadly, it seemed this wasn't a problem he could solve with fangs and a swirl of the metaphorical cape. Perhaps he had to suck up disappointment like every other parent in town. And yet... how could he not give his daughter, his Robin, everything a child could possibly want? What was he to do? Did all first-time fathers feel so confused?

It began to drizzle, so he turned up his collar. The stores were dimming their lights, and shopping was done for the night. Feeling in need of companionship and understanding, he turned his steps toward Joe's bar at the Empire Hotel.

The muted lights and sepia tone of the Empire's walls gave the place the look of a vintage photograph. Joe had decorated with pine swags and twinkling lights, and a jazz version of holiday standards crooned beneath the din of conversation. The warmth of the place had Alessandro unwinding his muffler before the door had fully closed. Already he was imagining Joe's special winter drink for vampires, filled with spices, blood, and brandy, warmed to the perfect temperature. The menu called it the Empire Bites Back.

Perry was chatting with Joe at the bar. Alessandro took the stool next to the wolf. Perry jumped slightly and spun around, his eyes flaring wolf-gold. "You've got to stop sneaking up on people."

Alessandro raised a brow while Joe laughed. "Something hot?" the bartender asked.

Alessandro nodded. "Thank you."

They chatted while Joe worked his magic behind the bar, somehow keeping track of half-a-dozen conversations while mixing complicated drinks. Alessandro's arrived with a sprig of plastic mistletoe on the rim of the mug.

Perry told him about an excursion to a craft fair and the demon-summoning children he found there. 'It seems sparkly purple things are catnip to tiny fae girls. Since they began this escapade, that might explain why the slime looked the way it did."

"Frederick the Unicorn has purple sparkles," Alessandro replied.

Perry rubbed his brow. "It's sad I know what you're talking about. I hear there's limited-edition purple Frederick cookies as well, though I thankfully haven't encountered any."

Alessandro heaved a sigh. "I can't find Frederick anywhere."

Perry patted his shoulder. "There, there."

Joe reappeared, replacing Perry's empty beer glass with a full one. "I think the fact the demon had sparkles is significant. Perhaps our wants and needs influence how it manifests."

Perry picked at the bowl of potato chips on the bar. "That's very philosophical, Mr. Joe, but I've had too much beer to think that hard."

Alessandro said nothing, but Joe's remark made sense. Had those little girls shaped how the demon would show up in this world? Why not, if it thrived on emotions?

There was a reason the demon had appeared as his parents, the vision straight from the winter his mother had perished. There had been no celebrations that year, or for many after. If he'd been human, the trauma from those years would have landed him in therapy—at least, in this day and age. But vampires didn't talk about their human pasts, preferring to see themselves as newborns the moment they rose from their graves. He hadn't spoken of those events—not even to Holly.

On the positive side, he'd spared her many grim tales. On the negative, there were other things he actually wanted to share — the breathtaking mountains of his original home, his family's way of life, and the peerless love of his mother and siblings. In a strange way, the demon had given his childhood back to him by reviving those memories. His thoughts had been full of his human past ever since, the sadness and beauty mixing like the colors of a painting.

Maybe it was time to break the rules and let Holly in. It would only be fair to let her see the man as well as the vampire.

Joe was still holding court. "If the season was universally cheerful, a holiday demon would be no more terrifying than a Labrador puppy."

Perry pointed a potato chip at Joe. "Life sucks if you dwell on the bad stuff. Don't feed the demon."

"I think it's more complex than that." Joe wiped up Perry's crumbs.

"Only if you need it to be." The wolf swigged his beer. "My answer to a pack Christmas is pacing myself. I never go to more than half the events. Just because I need some breathing space doesn't mean I don't love my family."

Joe poured shots for the three of them. "Cheers to complicated families."

They drank, and Joe poured again. This time, it was Perry who raised his glass first. "Cheers to challenging women."

They drank, and Joe gave a sly smile. "There are rumors you may have settled your choice for a plus one to my party. Congrats on the breakthrough."

"Maybe." Perry's ears turned pink. "We'll see."

"Do kiss and tell," Joe said, filling the glasses for a third time.

Alessandro picked up his glass. "I give you all women, from

the youngest toddler to the eldest grandmother, complicated or otherwise. May no demon steal their sparkles."

"Not even Frederick?" Perry quipped.

"I never want to hear of Frederick again." The words came out with more of a snarl than Alessandro intended. "I am a hunter, but it has proven clever prey."

"Oh, come on," Perry said with a lopsided grin. "You've managed a vampire queen and her court for hundreds of years. You've got connections and resources most of us can only dream of. Use your skullduggery."

Alessandro caught his breath, even if he didn't need one. Perry was right. He was so right. Vampires had survived not just for their fearsome skills as predators, but because they were clever survivors. Undead alliances and investments spread everywhere, with a vampire at every boardroom table that mattered.

He'd been so focused on being as good as a human father, he'd undervalued what made him unique.

Alessandro rose. He would bag his tiny girl a unicorn before the night was over.

"Did I strike a nerve?" Perry asked cautiously.

Alessandro smiled, letting his fangs slip out for good measure. "Excuse me while I make a call."

CHAPTER 8

Happy holidays, listeners, this is Errata Jones on CSUP coming to you from the radio station that adds the super to supernatural. There's snow in the air at the U of F campus, so maybe you'll want to wear your stockings tonight instead of hanging them by the fire.

Only two more shopping days to go, and we've been talking gift-giving this hour. You've heard suggestions from our retail experts on what to get those hard-to-shop for people on your list. There's always one, isn't there? The vampire with centuries of clutter in his garage or the mermaid who needs everything waterproofed? We've had some great suggestions from you listeners out in radioland, but here's another. I know from direct and recent personal experience that the best gift out there is yourselves, dear darklings. Your company is unique and personal, and you don't need to keep the receipt.

JOE SLOWLY COAXED his SUV through the powdery white that coated the road. Snow wasn't unusual in these parts, but it lasted only a few days out of the year. Since he didn't get much practice driving in it, all his senses were on high alert. Cars weren't like horses, who knew enough to watch their footing.

It was still early, barely ten-thirty in the morning. That qualified as dawn to someone who'd served his last drink at four that morning, but he had errands to run. The holiday season was madness in the hospitality industry, and if he wanted to keep a personal appointment, something had to give—in this case, sleep. But there was something he had to do, even if it was doomed to failure. The outcome would be the same this year as it had been the last, and countless times between. Rituals came in all forms.

He stopped at a gas station, getting out and helping himself while the attendant wiped the steam from the fog-shrouded windows of his booth. The man made no move to venture into the snow, only peered out at Joe. He was just as happy not to have to interact. Away from the conviviality of the hotel, he could admit Christmas put him in a funk, and this year was no exception. Perhaps this was why the demon had fascinated him—talk of its hunger for Christmas memories hit close to home.

Everyone had demons, at least the personal kind. For him, the image of a cozy family unit was pure fiction. His family—all except his brother—had been dead and buried for centuries. His father's house was long gone. Even the name on his credit card wasn't his own. He'd changed the Eastern European spelling to something the locals could cope with. It was hard enough for a monster to fit in without folks stumbling over the unfamiliar accents of his name.

He turned off the highway and into the woodlands owned by Pack Silvertail. Almost immediately, the snow grew deeper as if the wolves had somehow arranged it that way. The SUV's motor rumbled and wheezed, but the fat tires did their job. Fresh flakes started to fall, and he flicked on the windshield wipers. He had miles to go before he reached his destination, but a slog through winter woods was nothing when one traveled in modern comfort.

Not like when he'd been young, back in the days where Báthory Erzsébet, the Bloody Lady of Čachtice, had soaked in the blood of two hundred virgins. Joe—Josef back then—and his brother, Viktor, had been soldiers in her household guard. The pay had been generous, if one didn't mind a mistress who was a vampire.

They'd had a different concept of employment in those days. The countess had made a gift of the brothers to the sorcerer, Atreus, as a token of her admiration. That had been the end of Joe's human life. One day, he'd been at work in his native Slovakia, then, all of a sudden, he was cursed to an eternity in perpetual darkness. Joe had found it difficult, but Viktor had gone mad. So had Atreus, and so, apparently, had Elizabeth back in her blood-soaked bathtub. Insanity was in vogue with that crowd.

Eventually, Joe had escaped and become a bartender. The tips weren't as good, but the body count was minimal. He was good at his new job, possibly because nobody's problems surprised him after what he'd seen. All the same, he wore the pleasant, smiling mask of the innkeeper like a knight's helmet. It kept him safe even as it suffocated.

The SUV finally rumbled up to a split-rail fence that enclosed a huge paddock. He switched off the motor and sat for a moment, listening to the chatter of birds. For a moment, he was tempted to pull out his phone and double check that morning's liquor order. Or maybe the staff schedule—he would take as many shifts as he could, but it would still be hard when so many of the workers wanted to be with their families over Christmas. But no, all that could wait. For now, he had just one job to do. His gut tightened at the thought of it.

He got out of the vehicle, sucking in a breath as the frigid air bit his skin. Pulling off his glove, he put his fingers to his lips and whistled. The sharp sound split the air, but nothing happened. Disappointed, relieved, Joe searched the blue shadows beneath the tall pines. A magpie swooped down, tried to stand on the thick, soft snow, and then flew off again when he started to sink. Joe whistled again, but the only reply came from the irritated bird, now perched in the trees.

With a heavy sigh, Joe swung his legs over the fence and trudged across the paddock. The snow was just high enough to seep in through the top of his boots. He kept going, his hands stuffed in his pockets and his mind on business back at the hotel. At long last, he reached the opposite side and found a path that led into the trees.

Deep out of sight was a house, or perhaps the proper term was log cabin. It was only a few rooms, with checked curtains and a lean-to covering a woodpile. After he knocked at the door, he barely waited. He just turned the handle and went in. Joe blinked, snow blind despite the glow of a wood stove. When he could finally see, his vision told him what his other senses already knew.

His brother, Viktor, sat slumped in a rocking chair in the far corner of the room, his elbows braced on his knees. For once, he was in human form, his dark hair as long and shaggy as his beard. He was only a year older than Joe, but he looked like the wild man from their native folk tales.

"Why are you hiding in here?" Joe asked in their native tongue.

Slowly, Viktor raised his head, caution in his dark eyes. "I knew you would come," he said miserably. The words were slow and a little slurred. Viktor didn't speak much these days.

Joe flinched inside, although he didn't show it. "I'm not here to make you sad."

"I knew you would come, and that you want me to go with you."

The worst part was Viktor was right. They'd been together for so long, as boys, as men, as prisoners in Atreus's kingdom of darkness. Viktor's absence was like a missing limb. But after his brother had been freed from captivity, the only safe place for him had been this remote corner of Pack Silvertail's land. His wits had slowly returned, but he would never be the same.

Joe pulled up a stool, then sat facing his brother. Gently, he put a hand on Viktor's knee. "I just want to talk."

A glint of humor crossed Viktor's face. "You always want to talk. You should try not talking for a change."

"What's that supposed to mean?"

A long silence followed. Joe unzipped his coat, sweltering in the warm cabin. The pack members kept an eye on the place, making sure there was fuel and food and basic housekeeping. They also ensured Viktor stayed securely confined to his acre of land. The only time he left was when Joe supervised his outings.

"This is my home," Viktor said. "I don't want to leave."

Joe stifled a huff of impatience. "Is it so wrong for me to invite my brother for a Christmas visit? I'm having a party with all of my friends. Don't you want to meet them?"

"You try so hard to be human."

"I am human. So are you. Don't forget that."

But Atreus had cursed them to make them better fighters. Sadly, the curse hadn't broken when the sorcerer died.

"We are beasts," Viktor said, shaking his head. "I feel it calling to me all the time. It's better if I just listen."

Joe felt it, too, but he drowned that voice in relentless work. "It's only for a night."

"But you want me to go back." An edge of a snarl crept into Viktor's tone. "You always do when you come here. Every time you come, you ask the same thing."

"Why shouldn't I?" Bewilderment crept through Joe. "I want you with me, brother."

Frustration seemed to grip Viktor then. He shook his head wildly, thumping a hand on his knee. "But I'm here. I'm always here. I'm always here when you want me."

"It won't be Christmas without you."

"Yes, it will."

"It won't be perfect."

Viktor raised his head again, finally meeting Joe's eyes. For the first time in years, his brother looked back, fully present. "Perfect is here. Viktor is here."

Without ceremony, Viktor rose, pushing past Joe to leave the cabin. Uncertain, Joe got to his feet and followed him outside. That had been the longest conversation they'd shared for years, but Joe wasn't sure what any of it meant.

Viktor walked a little distance into the snowy field, his face tilted up to the muted sunlight. There was a joyous quality to his stance, as if he might break into a dance. Joe trailed after his brother, confused about what he was supposed to do. Was their visit done? Should he get back into the SUV and drive away? Would his brother know enough to go back inside when he got cold?

Viktor lifted his arms, stretching them up as if reaching for the vast expanse of the sky. He spun to face Joe. "Stop thinking!"

Then his image shimmered, as if a watery veil had suddenly come between them. Joe swore, knowing he had lost. A moment later, Viktor had transformed into the giant shaggy canine that was his beast. This was no werewolf, sleek and swift. Viktor was a mountainous hound, big boned and covered in wild dark fur. Shreds of his clothes were scattered over the ground, destroyed and forgotten.

He spun to face Joe, his big pink tongue hanging out.

"Viktor..." Joe groaned. "This isn't solving anything."

But his brother ducked, his tail in the air, and clawed the drifts with his massive front paws. Then he spun, spraying snow with his nose and loping a few yards before he stopped and turned again. He wanted to play. Was begging for it, brother to brother.

Joe closed his eyes, awash in confusion. The curse was an enemy. Work was his defense. Happiness was having every one of his chosen family, especially his beloved brother, gathered around his table for a holiday meal. That represented order, victory over chaos, a sign he had survived and flourished.

Watching the cavorting mammoth of a dog, it was plain Joe wasn't getting his wish. Somewhere, that Christmas-themed demon was laughing. Joe had a sudden, deep desire to return to the SUV. He wasn't a good loser.

But maybe he hadn't lost at all. What had Perry said? *Life sucks if you dwell on the bad stuff. Don't feed the demon.* Maybe Viktor wasn't ready to make his way in a crowd, but he'd said, plain as day, that he was right there. He wanted Joe's company as much as Joe wanted his, just on his own terms. It was a different kind of perfect, but it was within Joe's grasp.

After a long moment. Joe stepped back into the cabin and shed his clothes. It was bitterly cold, and he gulped a deep breath before running barefoot and naked back into the snowy field. Then he surrendered to the transformation and his beast. It was a strange sensation, dissolving and remembering a four-legged form, but all at once, he was warm in his own coat, and the wild woods called like forgotten friends.

Joe sprinted across the snow, his tail high in the air. He barked, chasing his brother until he nearly caught Viktor's tail in his jaws. Then Viktor spun, jumping on him so they rolled over and over in the snow, paws and ears and muzzles caked with white. Joe sprang up and ran, starting the game all over again in the gently falling snow.

It was the best Christmas gift ever.

CHAPTER 9

Holly sat on the wide steps of the Church of Saint Agnes, enjoying the warmth of a sunbeam as it bathed the sheltered porch. The morning had seen snow, but the clouds had parted in the last few minutes, giving way to blue sky. Beside her, the double doors of the church hall stood open for the steady stream of people visiting the combination craft sale and food drive. Holly volunteered for the event every year, and had talked Ashe into babysitting so she could do it again. The food drive had become as much a holiday tradition as eggnog and candy canes.

This year's innovation was a lunch for the volunteers, donated by the Empire Hotel. Holly was watching for Joe's delivery truck, happy to be getting some fresh air. Inside, the tables were mobbed by last-minute bargain hunters. The merchandise wasn't professional enough for the Yuletide Holiday Market, but it was fairly priced. One booth had mittens and hats made by the ladies at the Golden Swans. She'd spotted a monstrous striped muffler that had to be Grandma's handiwork—no one else could make an iconic—and perhaps ironic—green, purple, and orange scarf like that.

Holly's phone dinged, and she fished it out of her pocket. It was a string of emojis from Ashe: a cat face, a wolf face, mistletoe, and a series of hearts. Frowning, Holly sent a gif of a monkey scratching its head in confusion.

Ashe's response followed: *Did you hear about P and E at the craft fair? There were hellhound witnesses.*

Whoa! That was interesting. Holly quickly texted back: *Gossiping again?*

Ashe replied: *I'm babysitting. The only relief is scandal or day drinking.*

Holly: *Don't give me that. You love playing with your niece.*

Ashe: *Of course. I'm sure she'll be the next Vincent van Gogh, judging by the floor.*

Just then, Joe's van pulled up to the curb. Pocketing her phone, Holly jogged down the steps to help unload the food. As Joe got out and opened the back, others arrived to lend a hand. It was a mixed bag of humans and shifters, which was no surprise. The food bank helped everyone, so everyone helped in return, Joe included. The Empire had recently joined a program that donated unsold food to homeless shelters rather than add it to the landfill.

Once everything was delivered, Holly walked Joe back to the van. He seemed in high spirits, as if all was right in his world. "Thanks for doing this," she said. "Everything smells delicious."

"I'm glad to be in a position to give back." Then he flashed a sunny grin. "It's also smart business, since most of the volunteers are my regulars."

"It's all about the goodwill," she said with a laugh. "Spiritual and economic."

"It's also the right thing to do." Joe stepped off the sidewalk and onto the grass, drawing her aside. Holly complied, letting him lead her to a wooden bench. The church garden still held a few late roses, tipped by frost but bright against the backdrop of greens and browns. Unlike the countryside, only a few patches of snow still lingered in the downtown.

"Before I go, let me run this by you," he said.

"Sure," she replied, taking a seat beside him.

"I've been thinking about this demon infestation. Perry said it reflected the tastes of the kids who summoned it. The purple sparkly part."

"That's right. What about it?" Holly asked in surprise. Joe was a great conversationalist, but this wasn't his usual subject matter.

"We think of demons as a species, something biology might explain even if we don't always understand how their DNA works."

"Sure."

"What if there's more to it?" Joe asked, turning on the seat to face her. "I've not been visited by this demon myself, but it's got me curious."

Holly nodded, waiting for him to go on.

Joe went on. "This manifestation you conquered gathers strength through our emotional experience. There has to be a reason for that."

Holly watched a crow hunting through the fallen leaves. "Plenty of demons have strange habits. Collector demons horde. Soul-eaters infect others with mindless hunger. How is this different?"

Joe's dark eyes met hers. "How much does the literal hellspawn and our private demons overlap?"

It was a good question, and she thought for a moment before she answered. "A demon is a distinct entity, but there's some truth that they—I don't know if they overlap, but they can act as reflections of our problems."

"Explain."

"When I performed the exorcism, it tried to turn my insecurities against me. That's how demons work—they find the crack in your foundation that allows them to worm their way inside."

"But you sent it on its way. You didn't let it in."

"I didn't let it stay. I recognized what it was doing."

"How did you get rid of it?" Joe's expression was intent.

"Brute force. The power of Spirit. As the ritual ended, I remembered my happiest Yule memories. They came back vividly." She released a breath. "The experience reminded me how much I love this time of year. More to the point, I remembered how much I'm loved, even if I don't check every box on the to-do list. It was actually pretty liberating."

"Of course." He nodded, smiling faintly. "Perhaps we need nightmares to make us understand joy. Maybe our holiday demon is a catalyst for Christmas revelations, whether it likes it or not."

Holly closed her eyes, letting his words and ideas sink in. They felt awkward, like peering through binoculars from the wrong side—yet, there was logic in them. "I think you just blew my mind."

Joe laughed softly as he rose from the bench. "I'm not just a pretty face. And I'm not necessarily correct, either. It's just a thought."

"What inspired it?"

"I remembered what it is to be grateful." He grinned again. "I hope your food drive is a huge success."

With that, he went back to his van, leaving Holly to ponder. Instead of returning to the hall, she struck out through the churchyard. Surrounded by a wrought-iron fence, it covered a city block dotted with trees and monuments nearly as old as the town. The sun was sinking, casting a gentle glow through the bare branches. In the distance, a handful of urban deer cropped the grass, the stag lifting its head to keep a watchful eye on pedestrians.

Flowers graced a few of the graves, sometimes an elaborate wreath. Other times, it could be a jug of simple chrysanthemums. She knew a number of the names on the headstones—one of the hazards of growing up in a relatively small town. One was a girl from her high school. She had died in a riding accident. Another—and this one weighed in Holly's stomach like a brick—had died in a haunted house before she could save him and his friends. It hadn't been her fault, but the guilt never quite went away.

She shivered, suddenly aware that dusk crept across the sky. Soon, the holiday lights would come on, turning the city into a fairyland. Now wasn't the time to dwell on dark things. She started back toward the building and warmth, Joe's theories churning in the back of her mind.

Holly stopped and glanced over her shoulder, not quite sure why she did. A wind had come up, swaying the branches of the twisted oak trees until they creaked and muttered to themselves. No one else walked between the graves, although she found herself double checking. Perhaps she had talked herself into a case of nerves.

Then the deer raised their heads as one and bounded north toward the university's forest lands. Holly spun, wondering what had spooked them. A moment later, crows spiraled into the air, cawing in alarm.

She felt, rather than saw, the answer as a tremor rolled through the earth, sending the last of the autumn leaves showering from the trees. Primal panic raced through her, and she began to run, searching for any kind of cover. People streamed from the church, forgetting every earthquake drill they'd ever done.

A gravestone toppled in Holly's path, forcing her to skid to a halt in a spray of loam. Then cracks forked through the ground, spreading and branching from beyond the church and across the graveyard, as fine and complicated as a web of nerves. They weren't openings in the earth, but streaks of light as bright as molten steel—and they were heading straight for her.

It was magic. Demon magic, not sparkly and purple, but ten

times as deadly because this was the real thing, not some reflection of a victim's desire. The gloves were off.

Someone had opened a portal, and the demon was back with a vengeance.

Holly's stomach dropped as the streaks arrowed her way. Was it here to punish her for the exorcism? She spun and bolted in the other direction, legs pumping with a speed she didn't normally possess. It was hard to run on the shaking earth, but panic kept her moving.

From the corner of her eye, she saw the colorful splash of the flowers on the graves. If the demon could use old greeting cards to feed on, weren't graves loaded with a thousand times more emotion? What about the buried remains? The last thing she wanted was to see the dead walk.

Great Hecate, Grandpa Tom was buried here. Everything about that thought was unbearable.

Dropping to her knees, she dug her hands into the trembling earth. She knew other graveyards better than this one, but there had to be a ley line nearby. The ground beneath Fairview was rich with golden streams of magnetic energy that pulsed with the magic of the earth's core.

Holly struggled against her panic, fighting to concentrate on something besides the speeding silver lines. Instead, her thoughts scattered like frightened birds, refusing to obey. Her insides felt hollow, as if terror had turned her into a ghost. She sucked in a breath, forced it out, then did it again. But even those few seconds were costly—she heard the crack of splitting granite as the shaking earth toppled another gravestone.

The sound snapped her to attention. Time to get serious. Squeezing her eyes shut, she leaned forward to plunge her magic into the cold, wet ground. The ley lines here were thin —rivulets rather than rivers—but she found one easily enough. To her mind's eye, it flowed like liquid gold, bubbling and swirling as it wound beneath the roots of the graveyard's oaks. She drew it up like a butterfly drinking nectar.

The power swelled inside her, leaving Holly giddy. She rose to her knees just as the bright, branching light all but touched the fabric of her jeans.

"Get lost!"

She pounded one palm flat on the ground, releasing golden power right into the demon's web of light. The two forms of energy were completely incompatible. The demon's tiny, molten veins flickered like a shorting fuse, giving bursts of silver, then gold, then nothing at all. Her nose filled with its familiar stink.

But Holly didn't stop there. She pushed the golden energy of the ley lines down its throat. When it had all it could take, she pushed more until it choked. Beneath the power, she could feel the pounding heat of its bestial rage. The exorcism had hurt—and so did this. Vengeance would come.

The tremors stopped, leaving everything in deathly silence.

The minty-death smell of the demon coated her throat. Holly hung her head, sweat trickling down her back. Somewhere in the distance, a car alarm began to beep.

When she fished her phone out of her pocket, she was relieved to see its circuits hadn't fried. She dialed Perry's number.

He answered right away. "Hello?"

"It's Holly. The demon is back."

"What?"

"You said it was three little fae girls who opened the portal for the demon? They were trying to summon the real Santa?"

"Yes."

Holly sank forward until she was nearly double, burying her face in her free hand. *Kids.*

"I stopped them," Perry said. "Or I thought I did."

"Find their parents," Holly said. Excess power still surged through her, leaving her dizzy and faintly sick. "They've done it again."

Perry swore. "The earth tremor."

"I knocked the demon down, but it's mad. It'll be back again."

There was a beat of horrified silence. "I'll come help."

"No, contact the fae. Nothing else matters until those girls stop opening freaking portals. Hurry." She hung up.

With no adult practitioner to control the demon, it roamed at will. Conventional banishment, even exorcism, had limited success when little mischief-makers kept overriding those spells. Until then, it was a game of demonic whack-a-mole. Holly got to her feet and sprinted for the church hall, her feet stumbling with exhaustion.

"Hey," a volunteer said. "What was that?"

"*Leave*," Holly said. "Get everyone out of here."

"Why?"

"Just do it," she snapped, putting an edge of magical command into her voice.

The volunteer obeyed. It wouldn't take long to close everything down, Holly guessed. The tremor had already sent most of the shoppers scrambling to check on their homes.

Just to be on the safe side, she entered the church itself. Most of the staff had been helping next door, but she would leave no chance that someone might have been injured by the tremor. She walked to the foot of the nave, her feet all but silent on the stone tiles. The vast, shadowy space seemed to be deserted.

"Hello?" she called. "Anyone here?"

A scrap of darkness stirred in the very last pew. She turned, expecting to find someone resting or perhaps in prayer. She was wrong. Demons could assume many shapes, but her witch's sight knew the blurry, featureless man-shape as the thing she'd exorcized once already. Her insides twisted with fear so strong she thought she might be sick.

There was a theory that demons, vampires, and other not-quite-living creatures couldn't walk on holy ground. In truth, mileage varied. This entity had not fully manifested, probably to minimize discomfort. At least it wasn't parading as some tortured figure from her past, because that would bring it fully into the physical world. Of course, it only took a moment of solidity to end her life.

"I told you to get out of here," she said, surprised to find her voice clear and calm.

"I'll run if you do," it said, voice mocking. "I like a good chase."

She could run. Perhaps she should, although it seemed to have no trouble finding her again. But more to the point, there were volunteers outside, still finding car keys and wrapping up the last of Joe's food to take home. If she left, would it turn on them? And then there was Robin, Grandma, and Alessandro. She couldn't protect anyone if she ran.

"I'm tired of you," she said, gripping the back of a pew to hide her shaking fingers. "Whatever your name is."

"I don't need one," it replied. "I belong to every one of you. I *am* every one of you."

"Horse feathers," she said, using one of Grandma's expressions. "You're a demon all right, but a wannabe small-time feeder. What kind of hellspawn possesses Christmas ornaments?"

"You know why I do what I do," it said in a silky, insinuating tone. "You know it gives me what I like. Memories of disappointment and loneliness and loss. Of wanting so much and achieving so little. It's the best time of the year for my kind."

"Get real." Holly longed to shrink back, but didn't dare. As long as it was focused on her, it left everyone else alone. "You were summoned by preschoolers. You're just our own neuroses pasted onto a third-rate flunky of doom."

"Have a care," it warned, not so mocking now.

But Holly was just warming up, spooling spells in her mind while she kept it distracted. She'd spent most of her power already, so she had to make her next attack count. "You're one part wish fulfillment and two parts seasonal-affective disorder.

You're the embarrassing uncle no one wants at the Yuletide dinner table. You're the regifted fruitcake."

The thing snarled and stretched, growing so tall and thin its head reached the vaulted ceiling. Holly furrowed her brow. "That's all the intimidation you've got? Elastic Guy?"

In a flash, it grew paper thin and sank into the floor. Holly skittered back, unsure what would happen next. A moment later, the molten silver light was back, running toward her like quicksilver between the seams of the flagstone floor.

Holly's nerve broke. She bolted, zigzagging her way around the pews and down the side aisle of the church. The demon dogged her heels, never letting her pull more than a few steps ahead. The church began to shake. She burst through a side door, then another, and found herself on a staircase. The silver had a harder time flowing upward, and she finally gained ground. But after a few flights, the stairs began coiling upward in a spiral. Holly had found the bell tower—and she'd stupidly run into a dead end. The only way out was to descend straight into the demon's path.

She kept climbing upward, her mind scrabbling for more options. At the top of the tower, there was a tiny room with large open windows that offered no protection from the wind. Holly leaned against the doorframe, her legs burning from the climb. In the center of the room hung the church's single bell, its rope dangling through a hole in the floor. There was nothing else there—no weapons, no escape, not even a chair to rest on. Finding the farthest corner, she slumped to the frigid floor. It was as good a place as any to make a stand.

Her cell phone rang. Numbly, mostly out of habit, she answered.

"Ms. Carver," said a deep, melodious voice she didn't recognize. "This is Soren-itai of Clan Thonau."

Thonau was a light fae clan. Holly sat up, her pulse jumping with sudden hope. "I need your help. There's a demon…"

"Your werewolf friend explained," he interrupted. "My profound apologies for my daughters' misbehavior. I strictly forbade them to engage in any more spells, but disciplining the young in an age-appropriate way requires treading a careful line. Unfortunately, they disobeyed me again."

The silver lines were creeping over the threshold. They were smoking and sizzling now, which meant the demon had chosen to endure the pain of sanctified ground. It had to be extremely angry, and all of that rage was directed her way. Holly got to her feet, the phone pressed to her ear.

"I get it. I'm a mom. The demon is just across the room."

There was an intake of breath, as if he finally understood the urgency of her need. When he spoke, it was with the universal tone of the outraged parent. "I swear this is the last time the demon will bother you."

The line went dead. Holly stuffed the phone in her pocket, forgetting the fae in the face of a more immediate problem. The silver veins had picked up speed now that they weren't climbing stairs. Unless she suddenly learned to fly out the tower window, she had to fight.

Now the silver was eight feet away, stinking and smoking but growing thicker, as if the demon was gathering itself for a last, punishing assault.

Six feet.

Four feet.

Holly had just enough power to buy herself a tiny reprieve. Pressing her hands to the floor, she screamed in defiance, releasing the last of her magic. The strength rushed out of her, leaving her gasping for breath. This was it. She had no more to give.

Horribly, the silver flared gold for a heartbeat, but barely slowed in its march across the floor. The trembling of the building deepened, making the bell swing and the windows rattle. Holly summoned the last of her will, pushing against the demon. Pain seared through her magic, wringing a cry from her throat.

And then a different presence joined the fight—one she'd never felt before, as solemn and untamed as the buck she'd seen beneath the trees. *Soren-itai,* she thought, and felt his acknowledgment. Through the meeting of their magic, she sensed a father, chagrined and apologetic, but wasting no time in his task.

Fae spellwork was entirely foreign to Holly, but their temporary alliance formed a mental bond. She caught a flash of wide-eyed children confessing their disobedience. Then of the demon's original entry point in the woods beyond their rural home. Holly understood how that piece of information gave Soren-itai leverage over the hellspawn. Invading demons always had some kind of tether to their homeworld, and the fae had hold of it— and of the combined power of his light fae clan.

With an audible tearing sound, the demon was ripped from the world. A scream of psychic rage made Holly clutch her head and sag to the floor. "Stop, please stop," she muttered, willing herself to survive the moment.

The portal slammed shut, the demon and its fury on the other side. A second later, the doorway was sealed. And sealed again. Then the portal was locked, warded, and made air tight with a psychic caulking that made Holly envious of the fey's technique.

That demon was *not* coming back. The magic of an entire fae clan had seen to it.

She felt Soren-itai's firm promise, his regret, and the immense love he had for those naughty girls. Then he slid away as swiftly as the deer disappearing into the woods.

She was alone.

Holly picked herself up off the floor. The shaking had stopped, and the building was silent except for the cold breeze whispering through the tower windows. She sat on the edge of a broad window frame, exhausted and oblivious to the cold. The world had reached the exact point of darkness where the streetlights came on, wreaths of green and gold lights framing the old-fashioned globes. One by one, they flashed to life down the streets, as if the holidays arrived on a tide.

Perhaps Joe was right about nightmares being a catalyst for joy. For the necessity of standing against the shadows that targeted every weakness. Without struggle, there would never be victory.

Holly followed that thought, then let it rest. No doubt there were more nuggets of wisdom there, but she was too tired to tease them out. After the fight she'd had, the simple beauty of the town left an ache in her throat. The lights reminded her of the joy in her life. And generosity. Camaraderie. There was a reason this time of year was celebrated in every civilization she could name. Everyone needed beauty and hope.

She stood, summoning a witch light to guide her down the stairs. As she passed, she rapped her knuckles against the bell. The solemn vibrations rippled through the night, chasing away the last of the demon's presence. When the sound faded, the darkness was sweet again.

Holly left then, eager to go join her family. She took out her phone and punched Alessandro's number, achingly grateful to know she was so very welcome in his life. He would take her into his arms, chase away every last trace of fear and darkness. The adventure was almost worth the trouble, just so he would make her forget it.

"Hi," she said. "You up? You wouldn't believe the day I've had."

azel Carver hugged her great-granddaughter as hard as she could. The little girl had wriggled into the armchair where Hazel sat, as warm and lively as any young animal. She smelled of baby shampoo and ice cream, her impossibly smooth skin a velvet touch against Hazel's cheek.

"Oof, you're getting heavy!" she exclaimed, setting her down on the floor.

Robin giggled, her cheeks pink and eyes bright. She wore tiny red rubber boots and overalls with a snowman on the bib. She'd be too cute for words right up until five minutes past her nap time.

"Yeah, Robin's an elephant," Ashe's daughter said cheerfully, tickling her cousin. Eden was a teenager now, with a nose ring and a blue streak in her hair. Like her mother, she had a brash attitude that protected a soft heart.

My two girls, Hazel thought. *This is the future of the Carver witches.* Their reality was so different from the one she'd shared with Rose and Ashton, but she was certain this generation would conquer it with aplomb. And, if she were reading the signs right,

Ashe and her new husband, Reynard, would be adding to the tribe. Everything was as it should be.

Holly emerged from Hazel's bedroom with the girls' coats. "Thanks for doing the handoff."

Ashe had left the girls with Hazel for an hour before Holly picked them up. It was Ashe's turn for a night off—although from Holly's tale about the demon in the churchyard, perhaps it should have been Holly taking a rest.

"You could leave Robin a while longer, you know," Hazel said as Holly began the physics puzzle of inserting a toddler into a snowsuit.

"It's all good," Holly said brightly. "Eden has movie night all planned for us."

"With pizza," Eden added. "No olives."

"One with olives, one without," Holly amended. "You'll just have to look before grabbing a slice this time."

Eden made a face, but picked up the bundled Robin. "I'll go wait for Uncle Alessandro downstairs. G'night, Grandma."

Eden kissed Hazel's cheek and carried Robin out the door, taking a storm of teenaged energy with her. Most of the time, she was like a thunderclap about to happen.

Laughing, Holly brushed the hair from her face. "I'm looking forward to a night where food is brought to me and someone else is making the entertainment choices."

Hazel rose from her chair and hugged her, remembering when this girl was no bigger than Robin. "You don't need to push yourself this hard. Everyone will still love you if you take a night off."

"I'm slowly figuring that out. I'll be fine. Sandro is staying home to play ringmaster."

"Good."

Holly bowed her head, fingers plucking at the zipper of her coat. "I don't know if I should mention this, but did you feel the earthquake today?"

"It rattled the dishes, but not much more. Why?"

"That was the demon, too."

Shock numbed Hazel, robbing her knees of strength. She sat back down. "That thing was stronger than we thought."

"Yes, but it's all done now. It won't be coming back. The fae made that absolutely clear."

The initial shock of the story was fading, and now concern took its place. "How are you still standing after battling that creature?"

"I'll get my beauty sleep tonight, trust me. There's Joe's party tomorrow night. Would you like us to pick you up?"

Hazel sat back, annoyed Holly had changed the subject. "I'm not sure I'm going. I'm old. Those things go too late for me."

Her granddaughter smiled, silently calling her bluff. "I'll give you a call tomorrow." Then, like Eden, she kissed Hazel's cheek and left, closing the door behind her.

The apartment suddenly seemed deserted. Hazel sighed, not certain if she felt relief or regret. Slowly, the silence took over, broken only by the faint murmur of the fireplace and the distant sound of music from another suite. She picked up the remote control for the television, then set it down, not quite done with the quiet.

The demon—the one that had made Tom's cards into a weapon—had made a final stand. She was glad Holly and that fae fellow had finally defeated it, but Hazel wouldn't have minded a piece of the action for herself. She picked up her cigarettes and prepared to light one, thinking about conjuring Tom's face in the smoke.

"You don't need to do that," he said.

She all but leaped up, heart pounding, but her joints betrayed her. Grabbing the chair back, she nearly toppled over before she found her balance.

He was there, wearing an older face than the demon had shown. He stood by the entrance to the kitchen, not quite blocking the glow of the overhead light. "Easy, girl," he said in an old, familiar way that made her heart tremble. "I'm just a dead person."

It was true. This was a ghost. Not a demon, but the shade of her own Tom. She stared, swallowing hard in an effort to find her voice. "Wh—why are you here?"

"There was a disturbance in the churchyard," he said. "It drew me back."

He took a step toward her. Like all ghosts, he seemed to move as if underwater, his limbs slow and graceful. Yet, she could make out the traces of his limp. It reassured her as nothing else could. "It's taken you long enough to put in an appearance," she said tartly.

"You were the one who promised to come to me," he reminded her with a smile. "It's nearly time, old girl."

Hazel wasn't afraid of death. No one had a handbook for the afterlife, but like anyone who had handled true magic, she had faith in the power of rebirth and forgiveness. Fear wasn't what made her hesitate.

"I'm sorry, Tom," she said. "I'm not quite ready."

He was close now, just a few feet away. She could have reached out for him, but she knew he had no solid form. Just as well—if he'd taken her hand, her resolve might have crumbled to dust.

"I know," he said. "You've never once been ready on time, not even for our first real date."

His gentle teasing was as good as any caress. She ducked her head, feeling warmth mantle her cheeks. Who knew that after so much living, she was still capable of a maidenly blush? "I'm thinking of the girls. I want to see Robin's first day at school and Eden's first young man. I want to meet Ashe's next baby and look into his eyes."

"His?"

"It's time for a boy, don't you think?" She met Tom's gaze,

feeling an ache building in her throat. His eyes had never lost that startling shade of blue. "There are things they need to know, especially Ashe and Holly. There's no one here to give them advice about raising witch children. And spells. I haven't finished teaching Holly, for all that she takes on."

Tom patted the air in a gesture he'd often used to calm her down. "They'll know what they need when the time comes. That's how it works, however greatly we treasure our own opinions."

She released an exasperated breath, though tears filled her eyes. "I know I promised to come to you."

He smiled slowly, almost sadly. "But you want to stay a little while yet."

"Do you mind?" she asked, suddenly tentative.

His eyes crinkled as he laughed. "No," he said. "I'm as curious as you are."

"Good." Suddenly very tired, she sank onto one end of the flowered sofa.

"You need to sleep," he said, concern creasing his brow.

"Don't go," she pleaded, all at once as unsure as the girl who'd found a soldier on her porch steps. "Please don't. Sit with me."

He did, putting one ghostly hand over hers until she succumbed to sleep. There, they dreamed together.

"I don't understand," Alessandro said in bewilderment.

Holly gave him a look. "I think it's very sweet you asked the vampire queen to mobilize her Undead minions. They found Robin a Frederick the Unicorn in record time."

Queen Omara had been as good as her word. The courier had arrived with eerie swiftness, the brown paper parcel addressed in Her Majesty's own hand. She'd used scarlet ink.

The paper lay in shreds beneath the gaily twinkling tree. Frederick himself goggled up at the branches, legs splayed as if he'd been shot. Robin was trying on the box like a hat. The box, in fact, was the real hit among her Christmas Eve presents.

"I looked everywhere for that toy." Alessandro said, a plaintive note in the words.

"I know."

"I want her to have the best of everything."

"Of course."

"Why isn't she playing with it?"

Holly patted his chest. "Don't worry about it. She'll get around to the actual toys eventually. We need to go."

Frowning, he tried to make peace with the powerless status of a mere parent. Then Robin cast the box aside and held up her arms. "Paaaa!"

"You see?" Holly said. "You're still her favorite toy."

He turned into a puddle of fanged mush.

SOMETIME LATER, they parked outside the Empire Hotel, finding the last available spot. It was Christmas Eve, but the neighborhood was hopping. There was a dance party down the street where the club had taken over raising funds for the food drive, and there was also Joe's event. He'd wanted to celebrate with his friends, and almost everyone had agreed to come.

Christmas cheer seemed to pour into the street. The sound echoing from the Empire was filled with laughter and music, and the windows were bright with colored lights. Aromas of rich food and drink scented the streets for a city block. Joe had outdone himself.

He greeted them at the door. "Best of the season!" He kissed Holly's cheek and slapped Alessandro's shoulder, then extended an arm toward the back of the room. "Please come in. I'm unveiling some of my restoration work."

Alessandro paused in surprise. Sure enough, Joe had opened up the double doors at the far end of the room, allowing the crowd to flow into the hotel's old ballroom. "That part of the hotel was shut up forty years ago."

"Not anymore. Follow me," Joe said, leading the way.

They did as they were told, admiring the restored marble finishes and parquet floors. The ballroom was enormous, which was a good thing. So many guests needed space to mingle in comfort.

"You did a fine job," Alessandro said, admiring the ornate plasterwork. "This looks much like I remember it."

"And it's a perfect occasion to use the space again," Holly added.

Joe was clearly pleased. "It's been a labor of love, and I wanted friends to enjoy it first."

"And we shall," Holly said. "But before we lose you to the crowd, I wanted to invite you to our place tomorrow night. I'm cooking a dinner."

"At the revered Carver house?" Joe grinned. "I'd not miss it for the world. I might be a bit late, though. I'm going to spend Christmas Day with Viktor."

He said the last almost shyly, as if there was more than a simple visit involved. There was no time to ponder it, though, because someone called Joe's name and he was gone.

They saw Lore and Talia, Ashe and Reynard, and even Perry kissing Errata Jones under the mistletoe. Grandma Carver didn't come after all, deciding instead to save her strength for the turkey dinner tomorrow night. Joe had been as good as his word and provided a supervised play area, where they left Robin with Eden and Talia.

"Do you suppose," Alessandro asked Holly, "that we could find a quiet room upstairs?"

"Those floors aren't open to the public," she replied, curiosity in her eyes. "What exactly did you have in mind?"

He gave an enigmatic smile. "We're not just the public; we're party guests." Taking her hand, he led her to a narrow door in the corner of the ballroom.

"Where does this go?" she asked. "It looks like a staff entrance."

"It is." He pulled her through, his ability to see in low light guiding him through the narrow corridor. Thankfully, the path was clear of cobwebs and construction debris.

"Where are we going?" Holly asked.

"Up these stairs," he said. "Don't worry, I remember where they go."

"Where they went during Prohibition, you mean," she grumbled. Still, she followed him with an eager step.

The door at the top opened onto the first floor of hotel rooms. Once, they had been the most elegant in town, and the ambient glow of the streetlights outside almost restored their splendor. The door to the corner suite stood open, and Alessandro ushered Holly inside.

The rooms were almost empty, with just a few antiques hiding under dust sheets. That didn't matter—it was the privacy of the place he wanted.

"Why are we here?" Holly asked patiently. "I hope it's not for a romantic interlude because there's no bed."

"That will come in good time," he said, meaning every word. "Right now, I find myself in the mood to give you your Christmas present. And please don't wear the box on your head."

She gave a slight smile. "Shouldn't it wait until we get home?"

"No," he said. "This place has the right atmosphere. There is history, but also discovery, a storied past and eager future both."

In truth, there was no box involved. He drew the envelope from the inside pocket of his jacket, then put it in her hands. He noticed she'd done her nails in a deep red that matched her strapless gown. The dress glistened in the uneven light flooding through the bare windows.

Holly studied the envelope, then glanced up with girlish

eagerness. A moment later, she was easing the card from the foil-lined paper. "What's this?"

"Open it."

He'd chosen a fancy greeting card to serve as wrapping. Inside were plane tickets.

"*Italy*," she exclaimed. "We're going on a holiday!"

"You definitely deserve it. I promise you weeks away from all the work you do, and as much or as little sightseeing as you choose."

"Thank you," she said softly, closing the card and then opening it again, as if she half-expected the tickets were a dream.

"I also thought perhaps it was time to show you where I was born."

He said it solemnly, though he said it with a smile. This trip abroad was significant for him. Perhaps vampires rarely spoke of their human lives, but now he had the privilege of loving a truly remarkable woman. The private corners of his heart were safe with her.

From her expression, she understood the rarity of the gift. "Thank you so very much. I can't say it often enough."

"Spring would be a pleasant time to go, but not too early. My village was in the mountains." He imagined it, the surrounding meadows wild and starred with flowers. From what he could tell, that bit of countryside was still untouched.

She wound her warm, living hands around his neck and drank him in, her mouth hot and sweet and soft. She was his woman, his life, the mother of his child. Holly herself was the greatest gift he could have ever asked for.

He held her there, in the dark, with the sound of happy laughter like a blessing on the night. Holly slipped an arm around his waist. "It's snowing again," she said, and so it was, with lazy, spiraling flakes that promised drifts by morning.

They watched out the window, contented, as more guests

arrived with shouts of greeting. Joe's party was just getting started.

The cathedral bells sounded through the snow—the varied chimes of Saint Andrew's, the single clear peal of Saint Agnes's. They were announcing midnight. Christmas was here.

Alessandro drew Holly close, pressing his lips to her hair. For the first time in a long while, he felt an affinity with the holiday celebrations. A vampire spent eternity in darkness in every way he could name. But now, with this woman, the underworld had lost its hold. The darkest night finally heralded returning hope.

"Shall we go celebrate?" he suggested.

She turned her face up to his, seeking his mouth one more time. Then, after a pleasant delay, Holly took his hand. "Sure."

Together, they went back to the party and into the light.

THE END

AFTERWORD

Thank you so much for reading *Gifted* and stepping into my story world for a time. While you're immersed in the book, you're helping to create the place and people with your imagination. I hope this journey together was fun!

If you enjoyed the story, please tell a friend or leave a review. Reviews help other readers find good stories and are incredibly important to authors as feedback and in sales ranking and marketing. Your opinion matters!

Also, if you'd like to keep up on what's happening with my books, please sign up for my newsletter at

<u>www.SharonAshwood.com</u>

I promise that I won't share your email or information, and I won't send you spam. Around once a month I'll send you an email with contests, new releases, and previews of what's coming.

If you'd like to see more of the Dark Forgotten world, turn the page and find out how the series started with *Ravenous*. Holly Carver is a small-time witch who busts ghosts for tuition money, but ends up wrangling a demon when a haunted house job goes bad. Her Undead business associate, Alessandro Caravelli, suspects the demon is somebody's not-so-secret weapon. The supernatural community is at war, and Holly's unpredictable magic holds the key to the doorway to the demon realms. Soon Holly is on everyone's must have list, and not in a good way...

RAVENOUS

THE DARK FORGOTTEN

by Sharon Ashwood

Copyright © 2009 and 2017

Three Sisters Agency

 *Specializing in removal of*

*Hauntings * Poltergeists * Unwanted Imps*

Keep your house happy, healthy & human-friendly!
Best in the Pacific Northwest!

Holly Carver, Registered Witch

"Why didn't you say you were calling about the old Flanders place?" Holly's words were hushed in the street's empty darkness.

Steve Raglan, her client, pulled off his cap and scratched the back of his head, the gesture sheepish yet defiant. "Would it have made a difference?"

"I'd have changed my quote."

"Thought so."

"Uh-huh. I'm not giving a final cost estimate until I see inside." She let a smidgen of rising anxiety color her voice. "Why exactly did you buy this place?"

He didn't answer.

From where they stood at the curb, the streetlights showed

enough of the property to work up a good case of dread. Three stories of Victorian elegance had crumbled to Gothic cliché. The house should have fit into the commercial bustle at the edge of the Fairview campus, where century-old homes served as offices, cafés, or studios, but it sat vacant. During business hours, the area had a Bohemian charm. This place... not so much. Not in broad daylight, and especially not at night.

Gables and dormers sprouted at odd angles from the roof, black against the moon-hazed clouds. Pillars framed the shadowed maw of the entryway, and plywood covered an upstairs window like an eye patch. A real character place, all right.

"So," said Raglan, sounding a bit nervous himself, "can you kick its haunted butt?"

Holly choked down a wash of irritation. She was a witch, not a SWAT team. "I'll have to go in and take a look around." She loved most of her job, but she hated house work, and that didn't mean dusting. Some old places were smart, and neutralizing them was a dangerous, tricky business. They wanted to make you dinner in all the wrong ways. Lucky for Raglan, she needed tuition money. Badly. Tomorrow was the deadline to pay.

The chill September air was heavy with the tang of the ocean. Wind rustled the chestnut trees that lined the cramped street, sending an early fall of leaves scuttling along the gutters. The sound made Holly twitch, her nerves playing games. If she'd had more time, she'd have come back to do the job when it was bright and sunny.

"Just pull its plug. I can't close the sale with it going all Amityville on the buyers," Raglan said. Fortyish, he wore a fretful expression, a plaid flannel shirt, and sweatpants with a rip in one thigh. Crossing his arms, he leaned like limp celery against his white SUV.

She had to ask again. "So why on earth *did* you buy this house?"

Raglan peeled himself off the door of the vehicle, taking a

hesitant step toward the property. "It was on the market real cheap. One of those Phi Beta Feta Cheese frats was looking for a place. Thought I could fix it up for next to nothing and flip it to them. A little paint, fix the broken windows. Nothing fancy. Undergrads don't care about looks, as long as there's plenty of room for a kegger."

He dug in his pocket and handed her a fold of bills. "Here's your deposit."

Prompt payment—heck, *advance* payment—was unprecedented, un-Raglanish behavior. She usually had to beg. Holly stared at the money, not sure what to say, but she took it. *He's worried. He's never worried.* Then again, this was his first rogue house. Before this, he'd only ever called her to bust plain old ghosts.

He looked her up and down. "So, don't you have any, like, gear? Equipment?"

"Don't need much for this kind of job." She saw herself through his eyes—a short woman, mid-twenties, in jeans and sneakers, who drove a rusty old Hyundai. No magic wand, no ray guns, no *Men in Black* couture. Well, house busting—house taming… whatever—wasn't like in the movies. Tech toys weren't going to help.

She did have one prop. Holly pulled an elastic from the pocket of her Windbreaker and scraped her long brown hair into a ponytail. The elastic was her uniform. When the hair was back, she was working.

"Surely you knew the Flanders house has a history of incidents," she said. "The real estate companies have to disclose when a property has… um… issues." Holly eyeballed the place, eerily certain it was eyeballing her back. As far as she knew, Raglan was the first to hire someone to de-spook this house. No one else had stuck around long enough to pony up the cash.

Not a good sign.

Maybe next summer I should try dishwashing for tuition money.

Raglan blew out his cheeks in a sigh, fiddling with a thread on his cuff. "I thought the whole haunted thing wouldn't matter. The kids from the fraternity thought it was cool. Silly bastards. The sale was all but a done deal up until yesterday."

Holly walked up to the fence and put one hand on the carved gatepost. The flaking paint felt rough on her fingers, the wood beneath crumbly with age. The house had a bad attitude, but still the neglect made her sad. The old place had been built from magic by a clan of witches, just like Holly's ancestors had built her home.

Houses like these were part of the family, halfway to sentience. They lived on the free-floating vitality that surrounded any busy witch household—the life, the activity, and especially the magic. It was that energy that kept them conscious. Take it away, and the result was a slow decline until they were nothing more than wood and brick.

Reports of abandoned, half-sentient houses came up every few years. Centuries of persecution, combined with a low birth rate, had taken their toll on the witches. There were only a dozen clans left in all of North America, most with a scant handful of survivors. As their population dwindled, their houses perished, too. Most of these old, dying places were just restless, but a few turned bad, fighting to survive.

Like this one. Only its designation as a historical landmark had saved it from demolition.

Holly's pity mixed with a lick of fear. A gentle tugging was trying to urge her through the gate. Gusts of chittering whispers draped over her body like an invisible shawl. A caress, of sorts. The mad old place was inviting her in, embracing her.

Come in, little girl. So lively, so sweet.

A starved house would drain power from any living person, leaving them tired and achy. A magic user, especially a witch, was especially vulnerable. They had so much more to take.

A flush prickled Holly's skin as her heart sped up, filling her mouth with the coppery taste of fright. The strain of keeping still, resisting the whispers, made her teeth hurt.

Come in, little girl. The path to the front door was just flagstones buried in moss and weeds, but to Holly's sight it glowed. It was the one path, the only important route she would ever take. *Follow it and everything will be better. You'll be coming home at last. Holly, my dear, come to me.*

Holly pulled her hand off the post, putting a few paces between her feet and the property line. Sweat plastered her shirt to her back.

A hand touched her sleeve, but she didn't jump. That particular pressure, the curve of those fingers, was familiar, expected. Instead her heart skittered with a roller-coaster swoop of bad-for-you pleasure.

"I didn't hear you arrive," she said, turning and looking up.

Alessandro Caravelli was about six foot two, most of that long, lean legs. Curling wheat-blond hair fell past his collar, framing a long, strong-boned face that made Holly dream of fallen angels. The leather coat he wore had the scuffed, squashed look of an old favorite.

"I think the house had you." His voice still held faint traces of his native Italian, a slight warmth in the vowels. "I called your name, but you didn't hear me. I was crushed."

"Your ego's hardier than that."

"You make me sound conceited."

"You're a vampire. You're in a league of your own."

"True, and so is my ego." Alessandro gave a close-lipped smile that both invested meaning and denied it.

Holly pressed his hand where it rested on her sleeve, keeping the gesture light. Her pulse skipped at the coolness of his skin. Touching him was like petting a tiger or a wolf, fascinating but fearsome. Full of deadly secrets.

Some thrills were bad news. Working with a vampire was chancy enough; anything more would be insane. Besides, she already had a boyfriend—one who didn't bite. Still, that didn't stop the occasional soft-focus fantasy about Alessandro, involving satin sheets and whipped cream.

"So, this is the big, bad house on the menu," she said. *There goes the food imagery again.*

Dark as it was, Alessandro still wore shades. Now he slid them off, folding them with a flick of his wrist. The gesture was smooth as the swipe of a cat's paw, revealing eyes the same gold-shot brown as Baltic amber. He studied the Flanders property for a long moment, his face somber. Even after a year's acquaintance, he wasn't easy to read.

"Is this going to be difficult?" he said at last.

"No cakewalk. Raglan actually paid me the deposit already. He's afraid."

The sound of a car door opening made them both turn around. Raglan was standing by Alessandro's vehicle, peering in through the driver's side. The car was a sixties American dream machine, a red two-door T-Bird with custom chrome and smoked windows. Holly felt Alessandro coil like a startled cat. Where the car was concerned, he didn't share well.

The round headlights blinked on and off in an impertinent wink as Raglan fiddled with the dash. Alessandro always left the thing unlocked and half the time never removed the keys. To the vampire way of thinking, the car was his. No one would dare touch it. Until now he had been correct.

Raglan backed out of the car and slammed the door. "Sweet ride." Tension rolled off him as he skipped away from the car and gave a sheepish grin. He was acting out like a nervous little kid.

Alessandro made a sound just this side of a snarl.

Holly gripped his arm. "Not now. I need this job."

"Only for you," he said in a voice that whispered of cold, dead places. "But if he touches her again, he's dead."

Raglan cleared his throat. "Is this your partner? Pleased to meet you." He drew near but warily kept Holly between him and the vampire.

Alessandro gave an evil smile, but Holly poked him before he could speak.

Oblivious, Raglan cast a glance at the house, and his expression went from strained to about-to-implode. "So, what now? Can you get started?"

"I'd like to check one thing first. You mentioned that something happened yesterday, something that made you call me," she said. "Can you tell us what, exactly? We need the specifics."

"Yeah, well, I started work on the place, but it gave me the creeps. I kept finding reasons not to keep working. Then came yesterday." Raglan trailed off, his voice shaking. "Like I was saying, yesterday things went wrong."

Foreboding fondled the nape of Holly's neck.

Raglan hesitated a beat before going on, shutting his eyes. "From what I hear, four frat boys went in late yesterday afternoon for an end-of-vacation party. Not supposed to, because the final papers aren't signed yet, but they forced a window. Wanted to start christening the place, I guess. They never came out."

"Maybe they're still in there, sleeping it off?" Holly said hopefully. She knew denial was pointless, but it was traditional. Someone had to do it.

Raglan shook his head. "There's more to it than that. The police have already been around asking questions."

"The police?" Holly said, startled.

"They went through the house this afternoon, but didn't find a thing. The cops were spooked as hell, but there was no sign of the boys. That's when I called you."

"I can't help you if this is an open police investigation! Not without their permission."

"Please, Ms. Carver." Raglan wiped his mouth with the back of his sleeve, as if he were fighting nausea. "I'll never sell this place. I don't even dare go in it!"

A spike of anger took her breath away. Her voice turned to granite. "You didn't tell me any of this when you offered the job."

Raglan went on. "Two more people went in this morning, some of the professors who were supposed to be, uh, academic sponsors for the fraternity. They never came out either. The department heads called the dean to complain."

"Six people have disappeared inside that house? Since yesterday? *You couldn't have mentioned this on the phone?*" She felt Alessandro's hand on her back, steadying her.

Raglan sucked in air as though he'd forgotten to breathe for a while. "Ms. Carver, you've got to get those people out of there."

"You're right," said Holly, her voice thick. *The house is hungry.*

"Two questions, Raglan," asked Alessandro, his words quiet and chill. "How did the department heads know what happened? Who called the police?"

"Witnesses," Raglan replied. "Neighbors saw the kids climbing in through the window. And then there was the screaming."

Dragon Lords novellas

Lord Dragon's Conquest

Valkyrie's Conquest

Audiobook

Enchanted Warrior

Corsair's Cove miniseries

Kiss in the Dark

Secret Seed

Long Road Home

ABOUT THE AUTHOR

USA Today Bestselling author Sharon Ashwood is a novelist, desk jockey and enthusiast for the weird and spooky. She has an English literature degree but works as a finance geek. Interests include growing her to-be-read pile and playing with the toy graveyard on her desk. As a vegetarian, she freely admits the whole vampire/werewolf lifestyle would never work out, so she writes her adventures instead.

Sharon is a winner of the RITA® Award for Paranormal Romance. She lives in the Pacific Northwest and is owned by two naughty black cats.

www.SharonAshwood.com
Sharon@SharonAshwood.com

facebook.com/authorsharonashwood
twitter.com/RowanAshArt
instagram.com/rowanashart
bookbub.com/authors/sharon-ashwood
goodreads.com/Sharon_Ashwood
pinterest.com/rowanashart